A
Harlequin
Romance

ON A MAY MORNING

by

HILDA NICKSON

———————————————————

HARLEQUIN   BOOKS

Toronto • Canada   New York • New York

———————————————————

ON A MAY MORNING

First published in 1970 by Mills & Boon Limited,
17-19 Foley Street, London, England.

Harlequin Canadian edition published April, 1971
Harlequin U.S. edition published July, 1971

CHAPTER I

Her bare feet sinking into the creamy-white carpet of her room, Kate padded across to the large window and stood gazing out on to the scene she had known since childhood—the wide expanse of water, one of many which resembled lakes, but in Norfolk were called Broads. Broads, because unlike lakes, they were man-made, a result of the digging out of peat for fuel, many, many years ago. The hollows, in time, had become filled naturally with rain and for hundreds of years had lain forgotten, screened by the growth of trees and bushes, or hidden among marshes, the water gradually becoming overgrown with weeds and reeds.

Now, having been rediscovered, connected with the rivers and dredged, the Broads formed a system of navigable inland lakes which were a delight and relaxation for many thousands of people.

Kate gave a sigh of ecstasy at the sheer beauty of the morning and of the scene before her. Cocksfoot Broad, dredged and restored mainly by her father, lay enveloped in the pearly mist of a May morning, the green fringe of trees outlined like distant sentinels, the tall spire of the village church aloof but benevolent; and wrapped in peaceful slumber, two large motor cruisers quietly moored. At the staithe in the foreground were river craft of all kinds. Yachts, day boats, dinghies, launches, cruisers of all sizes, houseboats—which were called Flats Afloat, the occasional rowing boat, and her own half-decker, the *Aerial*.

A contented smile curved Kate's lips. It was all very satisfying and she loved it. Her father's boathire business was one of the biggest and most prosperous in Broad-land, and had a most advantageous position as well as

5

having a pleasant outlook. Now the golden rays of the sun began to pierce the mist and Kate experienced a sudden thrill of excitement, a feeling as if something wonderful were about to happen. She glanced at her bedroom clock. It would be a full hour before her father would waken, and another half on top of that before he would want his breakfast.

Swiftly she pulled on slacks and a sweater and thrust her feet into a pair of canvas shoes, barely making a sound as she hurried down the stairs and snatched up an apple from the dining room sideboard. She would do what she had not done for ages—go for an early morning row.

Pausing only long enough to pick up a pair of oars from the small boat shed, she ran along the quayside to where the *Aerial* was moored. With this boat she had the best of all worlds in sailing. A lug sail, managed easily single-handedly, an engine to help her out of difficulties or speed the way home, a canvas awning for'ard in case of heavy showers, and when required, was fairly easy to row.

She let go both moorings and gently dipped the oars into the water. Not a soul stirred and within a few minutes the mist had parted and closed up again to admit her into a milky-white world apart. She rowed effortlessly, allowing the boat to make maximum use of its own 'way' between each pull of the oars, savouring the exquisite peace and serenity only to be found on the river on a morning such as this. She kept to the edge of the Broad where the reeds grew thickly, knowing that if she adhered to this course she would come to the cut which led to the open river. Vaguely in her mind was the idea that there, in about half an hour's time, there might be enough breeze for a short sail. In spite of the ever growing popular demand for motor cruisers, she still preferred sailing to power, providing conditions were right.

6

At the mouth of the Broad there was an overgrown creek which led to a large empty house called the Grange. The owner had died a few years ago and there had been some difficulty in tracing the next of kin. All kinds of rumours arose from time to time—one, that the next of kin was a nephew and that he was living abroad, another that he was married and that his wife did not want to live in Norfolk, yet again that he was a bachelor and intended selling the house, and more recently that the place was derelict and was to be sold as a building plot.

All at once Kate was consumed with curiosity to have a look at the house. The previous owner had always kept a barrier across the inlet in the form of a rail and this was still in position, although it was extremely doubtful if any wandering Broads holiday-maker would have ventured to thrust a way through the overgrowth. Kate's boat was small compared with most of the hire craft, however, and she decided to try. She shipped her oars and after a struggle managed to lift the barrier and fight her way through the reeds, weed growth and brambles. There did not seem much point in replacing the barrier.

But as she pushed her way through the blanket weed and rounded a bend she was surprised to discover how clear was the rest of the creek. Still out of actual sight of the house, even though rowing meant having her back to it, she made progress easily, and wondered how much truth there was in any of the rumours.

The previous owner had been a retired major-general, an unfriendly, crotchety person. Kate remembered how he had once shouted at her from the bank when she was a child for venturing up here. He had brandished his stick at her and shouted:

'Don't you know this is private property? Don't you dare come up here again, do you hear?'

It was from that time on that he had put up the barrier, and Kate had never trespassed again. She had never wanted to. She had been far too busy helping her father with his business to bother about the Major-General.

She smiled suddenly at the sight of a pair of swans and their four fluffy-grey cygnets. She had always suspected that there was a nest up here. Knowing how jealously they guarded their young, Kate gave an extra pull on her right-hand oar to skirt as far away from them as possible. As it was, the male swan advanced menacingly, its wings arched, its neck thrust forward to make a distinct hiss. No need for panic, but no point in annoying him.

Kate gave one or two strong pulls and sent the half-decker skimming through the mist. She was a good straight rower and at this hour of the morning, up this particular creek she did not need to keep glancing over her shoulder. There would be no other craft about. However, she was just about to do so, thinking she must be somewhere near the end of the creek and should now be able to see the house, when she felt a sudden impact, and at the same time a voice sounding very much like that of the late Major-General called out:

'Watch out there, can't you?'

Kate slewed her head sharply and saw a man in a rowing dinghy, his face furious.

'I'm sorry. I—I didn't expect anyone to be up here.'

'Obviously. Don't you know this is a private water-way?'

Now he sounded more like the Major-General than ever. 'Yes, I do know as it happens, but—'

'Then I suggest you remember it in future. I suppose you thought the barrier across the entrance was just for decoration?'

Kate stared at him. It was a very long time since she had met anyone so rude and unfriendly in this part of the country. Could this be the nephew of the rumours? He was not young, at least, not as young as herself, but he was not middle-aged either. Just a man—with dark

8

brown hair. Could even be good-looking, she supposed, if he were not scowling so heavily. But she had no time for people who would neither accept an apology nor listen to explanations. All the same she was determined he was not going to be allowed to get away with such rudeness without some retaliation.

Making sure by a swift glance that she had not really damaged his boat, she dipped one oar into the water and began to turn the half-decker around.

'May I take it that you are the new owner of the Grange?' she asked icily.

'You may.'

'Then nothing would ever induce me to come up here again,' she flung out, '—whether there's a barrier at the entrance or whether there isn't!'

She rowed swiftly back the way she had come, her enjoyment of the morning spoilt. What an unpleasant, overbearing man! She hoped she would never have to meet him again, in spite of their being near neighbours. She made her way through the weed growth at the entrance, making sure to replace the barrier rail, then turned into the Broad again. She did not feel like hoisting sail now, even if there had been sufficient breeze.

But now the sun was warm on her back and it was not long before her good humour was restored at least in part. Her father and herself had seen very little of the Major-General when he had lived at the Grange. There was no reason why his nephew should trouble them very much either—if nephew he was, which seemed very likely, judging from his obnoxious manner. But she could not dismiss the man from her mind entirely.

Kate had been out longer than she thought. Some of the holiday-makers aboard the moored craft and the houseboats were already taking in the morning air as she tied up her own boat and when she entered the house her father was already up. He was in the breakfast

9

room reading the morning paper.

'Hello, Father—you're up early.' She dropped a light kiss on his cheek.

He glanced up briefly. 'So are you. Where on earth have you been?'

'Oh, just for a row. It was such a lovely morning. I'll pop upstairs and have a wash before I get breakfast. I won't be a jiffy.' At the door she paused. 'The paper's early, too. How did that come about?'

'I went to the station for them myself. I get a little tired of waiting for Joe to bring them.'

Kate went upstairs, vaguely disturbed about her father. He had not been quite himself lately. He had been restless, somehow, flew off the handle easily, seemed tired more often than he used to be. He was normally so full of energy and drive, able to cope with anything and still remain cheerful.

She passed his room, and through the half-open door caught sight of the photograph of her mother which had been on his dressing table ever since she could remember —except that from time to time he bought a new frame for it.

Poor Daddy, she thought involuntarily as she splashed water on her face. Though he had never shown it to the outside world, and seldom, in actual fact, to herself, he must have missed his wife terribly. Theirs had been a very romantic story. They had met while they were on holiday on the Broads and had fallen in love almost at first sight. Both had a little capital—her mother a small legacy, her father a gratuity from the Navy—so they decided to start a boathire business. Cocksfoot Broad in those days had been badly silted up, only a narrow channel in the centre fit for navigation, and that only for small boats. But on the site were two houses attached to each other, a huge barn and plenty of land. Looking into the future, Eric Martham saw it as ideal both as a place to live and a site for a boatyard. The two houses were knocked into one, the barn used as their first boathouse, and each year more and more dredging done until the Broad was now the wide, clear expanse it was today.

Tragically, soon after Kate, their first child, had been born, his wife had died of a heart condition which, these days, would undoubtedly have been cured by operation.

Kate brushed her short hair swiftly. Her father had never ceased to talk about her mother.

'Your mother would have liked that,' he would say, time and time again. Or: 'Your mother *would* have been pleased,' when they had had a particularly successful year, or when they had added yet another boat to their fleet. Yet again a few years ago when a shop, and milk bar and small café had been added for the use of visitors.

Kate hurried downstairs, and with an ease born of long practice, soon had breakfast under way. Assisted by a daily woman, she had kept house ever since she was fifteeen as well as helping with the business, and had been happy doing it. Her father made her a generous allowance which he called salary, and with the highly successful business there had never been any lack of money for the small luxuries of life.

She loaded a trolley on which stood a hotplate to keep the bacon and eggs warm and wheeled it into the breakfast room.

Eric Martham looked up from his paper irritably. 'These jumped-up idealists make me sick!' he exploded.

'Why, Father? What's the matter?' she asked, pouring out the coffee and placing cornflakes and milk to hand for him.

'An article in this morning's paper, by somebody called Thornton. Just as the Broads Report looks like being accepted and something might get done to ease the congestion—if there is any—some so-called expert 'points out' that even if more boatyards were built on the south rivers and more Broads made, boat-hirers would still flock to the north to congested places like Horning and Wroxham, and even suggests sarcastically that fairy lights might be slung between the proposed landscaped trees.'

'Fairy lights!' Kate burst out laughing. 'Well, it *would* look rather pretty.'

Her father folded the newspaper angrily and slapped it down on the table.

'It's no laughing matter. This maniac is actually talking about *restricting* the number of craft on the rivers. How ridiculous and unrealistic is it possible to get? The trouble is, half these bods who go around shooting their heads off and writing articles to the papers don't *know* the Broads, still less *use* them. Some of them don't even live in the area. Even in the height of the season I can take any one of these so-called experts to quiet mooring places they'd have all too themselves.'

'Yes, Father, that's true. Of course, there has to be an end to development some time, hasn't there? Otherwise the very reason for the Broads' popularity would be in jeopardy.'

Eric Martham eyed his daughter with a heavy frown. 'I've heard that one before, too. Whose side are you on, Katie, anyway?'

She looked at him in surprise. 'Whose side? Well—ours, yours and mine, of course.'

'I'm glad to hear it. And I want no more talk of restrictions. How far do you think we'd have got in the business, if somebody had imposed restrictions on the number of boats we could have for hire? There's still plenty of room on the Broads and rivers and plenty of scope for opening up more. All that's needed to make south of Yarmouth as picturesque and interesting as the north is to flood a few acres of marshland, dig out a few more Broads and plant some trees. It's as simple as that.

But some clever Dick of a maritime engineer or architect or whatever he calls himself besides Thornton starts being sarcastic and—'

Kate did not argue with her father. She was more concerned with him than with the subject under discussion. Something was making him much more irritable than he used to be. Did it really stem from the controversy started by the publication of the Broads Report? As usual there were extremist views on what should be done about the Broads, a holiday centre which was becoming more and more popular, in spite of an increasing number of people having the money for holidays abroad. In the main, she agreed with her father, naturally, but there were some aspects of the Report and its recommendations about which she had not quite made up her mind.

'Do you think an article like that will carry much weight?' she asked.

'Heaven knows. One thing's for sure—if there are a sufficient number of people stupid enough to allow themselves to be persuaded by people like this Thornton, and many more with his views, the Broads holiday industry is likely to be strangled. We've got enough troubles on our plate at the moment as it is, what with the speed limits on day launches and the new regulations about toilet facilities.'

'Yes.' Then thinking it would be better to get away from worrying subjects, Kate told her father about her encounter with the new owner of the Grange this morning, making no mention of the fact that he was rude to her, or of her answer to him.

Her father looked interested. 'What sort of a man was he?'

'We-ell, I can tell you what he looked like, but that's about all. Not expecting to find anyone else up there, I bumped into him—literally—and I don't think he was very pleased. An educated man, judging from his accent, possibly in his thirties. Tall, from what I could judge. Dark hair—the rugged outdoor type.'

' Mm. Well, I wish him joy of the Grange. It must be in a fine old state of dilapidation by now. Two or three years of unoccupation can wreak havoc on a house —and old man Bradley let the place go to rack and ruin anyway. Has he already taken up residence, then, this fellow?'

' I don't know. I asked him if he was the owner, and he said he was, so I turned around and came back home.'

' Well, I expect we shall be coming across him sooner or later if he's going to live here.'

Kate laughed. 'Perhaps Millie Thorpe will know something about him. She usually does. There's a girl works in her father's office who is a perfect mine of information. I shall be seeing her this evening.'

Eric Martham passed his cup across the table for more coffee with a sceptical grunt.

' That's the kind of information you have to take with a pinch of salt. Gossips make up half of it.'

Kate grinned. ' I expect you're right. All the same, if there is any information to be gleaned—'

' Are you interested—or just curious?' asked her father.

Kate shugged. ' Curious, that's all.'

Breakfast over, Eric Martham went outside to attend to one or two things in the boat sheds. Kate's routine was to clear away the breakfast things and stack them in the kitchen ready for Mrs Morgan, their daily help, when she came at nine o'clock, then make the beds and be in the boatyard office about nine.

As she cleared the table she picked up the paper and glanced through the article which had so incensed her father. It was certainly written in the most forthright terms. It spoke scathingly of Broads developers and the owners of large hire-fleets, accused them of destroying the character of Broadland in their greed to make more and more money, drew a picture of an unbroken procession of motor-boats passing between banks lined with chalets, shops and cafés, and—among other things—recommended the banning of houseboats.

Kate heaved a large sigh. No wonder her father had been so upset! Taken to heart, it made her father, along with men like Mr Faulkner, her father's friend, seem like money-grabbing creatures who cared nothing for the beauties of nature and were bent only on commercializing the Broads.

But it wasn't true, she thought defensively as she went about her work. What was the use of rivers and Broads if boats were not sailed on them, either yachts or motor cruisers? As to the houseboats moored along the banks, they added to the general character of Broadland. Through the enterprise of men like her father, thousands of people had been given a greater appreciation of the countryside. This man Thornton did not know what he was talking about. If she ever met him, she would tell him so.

Kate's day as usual, was divided between house and boatyard. Jill of all trades, she sometimes called herself, doing the cooking and housekeeping, lending a hand wherever it was needed most. In the office, the shop—which sold gifts as well as every item of food which one could mention—in the café, milk bar and around the boatyard, helping people to moor their craft or hiring out day boats, though work in the sheds and on the quayside was largely her father's job. But always, Kate's first task was to sort the mail.

After having a few words with Mrs Morgan, she went across to the office and opened and sorted the letters.

Some she passed on to Sheila, the typist, to answer, to others she dictated a reply on to tape, and one she put aside to consult her father about. She answered the telephone once or twice, then went along to the milk bar for a cup of coffee. To her surprise—as he was usually busy at this time of day—Jim Faulkner was there talking to her father. They both looked grim and Kate guessed they would be discussing the article in this morning's paper. They were sitting at a table not far from the counter, and as Kate approached to get herself a cup of coffee, her father glanced up and saw her and pushed his own cup toward her.

'Here, Katie, have this. I'll get myself another one.'

She thanked him and he stood up and went to the counter. Kate dropped into a seat.

'Good morning Mr Faulkner. Lovely day.'

'Morning, Kate. But not so good and not so lovely apart from the weather, which I must admit is pretty good for May.'

She smiled slightly. 'I expect you're upset about the article. I know Father was when he read it, and I must say I think it's a little unfair.'

'A little unfair! That's putting it mildly. Not that I'm worried about the opinions of people like that Thornton bloke—whoever he is; it's the influence on others that counts. I'm hoping to develop those mooring plots of mine just below Yarmouth. There's plenty of room there for a restaurant, a few chalets and a small boatyard. I've applied for planning permission, as I expect you know, and there's a meeting of Town and Country Planning in a few days' time. This article could make the difference between permission or refusal.'

'I can see your point, Mr Faulkner. It was a very persuasive article.'

Putting aside the injustice to men like her father and Mr Faulkner, there were aspects on which she felt even herself being persuaded. It was certainly true that if a sufficient number of people had Mr Faulkner's ideas there would soon be no part of the river bank which was not built upon. It was all a matter of balance. Some riverside houses with their well-kept, smooth green lawns sweeping down to the water's edge and their beautiful gardens added a great deal of charm to the scene, as did the ones which were thatched and half-timbered. But the bleak parts, such as the marshland areas, were also attractive, having a wild natural beauty all their own. There were some planners who would have even erected shops and restaurants on the banks of Breydon Water— that inland sea over four miles long which gave holiday skippers the feeling of cruising at sea, especially when a strong breeze produced choppiness. Norfolk's Broads had something for everyone, but some vigilance was necessary. Why did Mr Faulkner want another business on Broadland? she wondered. Like her father, he already owned a very large fleet of boats of all kinds as well as an inn called the Wherry which had a very nautical character and was very popular both with holiday-makers and residents.

But Mr Faulkner supplied the answer.

'It's not for myself, it's for Lance,' he was saying. 'He wants his own business when he gets married, not a share in mine.'

Did he? Kate wondered. Lance and herself had been friends for years. She had never heard him mention such an ambition.

Her father joined them, and Kate still felt he was worried about something out of all proportion to what might happen with regard to the business.

'Did you say you were going out tonight, Kate?' he asked.

She nodded. 'Lance is having a record session.'

Eric Martham sipped his coffee. 'Yes—well, come

over about eight, Jim, and we'll chew things over then. Maybe you'll leave some sandwiches, Kate.'

'Yes, of course,' she said, wondering what it could be that her father needed a whole evening—or part, at any rate—to talk over with Mr Faulkner.

'I'll be glad to get away from the place if the kids are going to be playing pop records,' laughed Jim Faulkner. 'Doris will be out too. It's W.I. night.'

Kate made no reply to the reference to pop records. Lance's interest in that kind of music had waned a long time ago, the same as her own had. Now they preferred folk music and were gradually becoming more interested in the classics. Both she and Lance—and Millie, indeed, all of Kate's friends were long since out of their teens, but it was a complaint of most of them that their parents still treated them as children instead of adults.

During their evening meal Kate waited for her father to tell her what it was he and Lance's father wanted to talk about. She was sure it was more than an ordinary friendly chat. But he didn't. It surely couldn't be about Mr Faulkner's proposed new development, she thought. That had nothing to do with her father, and a man of Mr Faulkner's experience would hardly need to ask his friend's advice to the extent of spending an evening with him. But her father sat in a silence which became increasingly noticeable as the meal progressed. At last Kate asked him:

'Father, what's the matter?'

She startled him out of his thoughts. 'I'm sorry, Katie. Nothing's the matter, really.'

'But there is,' she insisted. 'You haven't been your-self for a week or so now. You're not worrying about the business, are you? You can't be. We're doing as well as ever and—'

He shook his head swiftly. 'No, no, it's not the business altogether, though that's worrying enough these days.' He sighed. 'To tell you the truth, I—' he broke off and shook his head. 'No, I can't. It's too silly for words.'

'What is? Come on, Father. You've got to tell me.'

He laughed briefly, then sighed again. 'I hadn't thought it showed. You'll never believe this, but—well, to tell you the truth, I'm still missing your mother quite a bit. It—was about this time of the year that we met. On a May morning just like this, as a matter of fact.'

'Oh, Daddy—'

Mingled sympathy and relief washed over her. She had been afraid it was something much more serious. She left her seat and went to put an arm around him, kissing his cheek.

He patted her shoulder. 'Go back and get on with your meal, girlie, it's all right. It gets me like this now and then. But it's nothing for you to worry about. As a matter of fact, *I* get a bit worried about *you* at times.'

'About me? Good heavens! What is there to worry you about me? I'm all right.'

'Maybe you are, but lots of girls your age are engaged to be married by now, and I'd like to see you with a decent man of your own before I—'

Kate laughed, but at the same time eyeing him a little anxiously. *Was* he ill and trying to keep it from her?

'But that's nothing for you to worry about. I've got heaps of time yet before I think of getting married.'

'Yes, I suppose so, but I don't want you getting any ideas of not wanting to leave me or any of that nonsense. You have your own life to live.'

Relief washed over her once more. 'Oh, I see. Well, don't worry, Father. When the right man comes along we'll work something out.'

'What about Lance? I'd have thought you and he—'

Kate screwed up her face. 'Oh, Lance is all right, and we're great friends, but I don't think either of us see each other in the light of life partners.'

Her father smiled. 'You've known each other too long, that's the trouble. One of these days you'll suddenly wake up to the fact that you're in love and have been for a long time.'

'You like him, do you, Father? You wouldn't mind him as a son-in-law?' she quizzed light-heartedly.

'Mind him? I think he'd be the ideal choice.'

Kate made some casual reply, relieved that he had only been thinking in a way natural to a father with an only child, and that child a daughter. Lance and herself did like the company of each other in preference to some others in their circle of friends, but they were not in love. At least, she mused, as she cleared away and set the kitchen to rights before going out, there were none of the signs of being in love she had heard about. No day-dreaming, no feverish haste to be with the other, no looking in shop windows at bridal outfits or furniture. And on Lance's part? He treated her too casually to be in love, and more important, he had never mentioned marriage.

Lance's parents had a house on the river Bure, employing a manager to look after their inn, the Wherry. It was a lovely old Georgian house, its lawn sloping down to the water's edge, the boatyard and sheds out of sight at the back, yet accessible by boat by means of inlets as well as by road. Kate took her own small car and drove the four miles along a minor road sprinkled with reed-thatched cottages, their gardens gay with red and yellow tulips, wallflowers and spring-flowering shrubs. She would not wish to live anywhere else in the world, she told herself.

When she arrived at the house, Millie Thorpe and one or two others were already there. As it was a fine evening and not too cold Lance had decided to have a barbecue supper and had set out canvas chairs, drinks and a record player on the wide patio overlooking the river.

Lance poured her out a drink. 'I understand our respective fathers are chewing something over. Any idea what it is?'

Kate shook her head. 'Haven't you?'

Lance ran his fingers through his thick fair hair and sighed.

'Because I still live at home and I'm not married—or about to be—he still thinks I'm a juvenile.'

'Oh, I wouldn't say that, Lance. You have to see it from his point of view. To the average parent it seems less than no time at all since we were born. Believe me, they know we're adult all right. I expect your father wants to ask mine for his advice or opinion about something—something he's already talked over with both you and your mother.'

They talked for a few more minutes about the business, then Millie extracted herself from the rest and joined them. As Kate fully expected, she already knew about the newcomer to the Grange.

'He's not exactly a stranger to the Broads area, but he's been living somewhere near Wymondham,' she told them.

'Are you sure?' queried Kate. 'I thought he was supposed to be Major-General Bradley's nephew who was abroad somewhere.'

Millie shook her head. 'Oh no, that was only rumour. This man hasn't anything to do with old Bradley.'

'You surprise me,' Kate said. 'I'd have said he was every inch a Major-General.'

'You mean you've already met him? What was he like?'

Kate told her about the encounter with him that morning. 'Admittedly I knocked into him, but I didn't do any damage to either him or his boat. And I suppose I could be said to have been trespassing—though it's a very moot point whether *any* waterway is strictly private unless it's a pool in somebody's garden. But anyone would have thought I was stealing apples from his orchard the way he carried on. So if you want to know what he was like, as far as I'm concerned he's bad-tempered, unsociable, unfriendly—'

'Wow! He has got you incensed, hasn't he?'

'I should think so, too,' said Lance. 'And if Kate was only rowing she couldn't have knocked him all that hard.'

'Did he know who you were?' asked Millie.

Kate laughed shortly. 'He didn't ask, nor give me a chance to tell him.'

'How odd. He doesn't sound like the same man I've been hearing about. They say this fellow from Wymond-ham—Leigh or something—is quite a man, and a very eligible bachelor.'

Lance raised his brows. 'And what, I would like to know, makes a man "a very eligible bachelor"?'

'Well, he's not my type,' Kate put in swiftly.

Lance put his arm across her shoulders. 'I'm your type, aren't I, Kate?'

She laughed and touched his nose affectionately. Yes, that's right, Lance.'

Millie shrugged. 'Well, congratulations, both of you. I'll dance at your wedding. Myself, I think we could *do* with a fresh face around these parts.'

She moved away and began to talk to someone else. Kate thought it most unlikely that the new arrival would become a part of the general social set-up in the area.

'He might even be married,' she said, unconsciously speaking her thoughts aloud.

'Who might?' asked Lance.

'The new owner of the Grange.'

'Oh, *him*.'

'He certainly looked old enough.'

Lance eyed her with some amusement. 'He seems to have aroused your interest, anyway.'

'Well, unpleasant people often do arouse one's interest, if you can call it that. It's just that they get you all worked up—like the man who wrote that controversial article in this morning's E.D.P.'

'Oh, you mean that fellow Thornton? He's a consultant or something, according to Father. But whoever he is, his ideas won't be very popular with the boat-owners. I thought he had a point or two, myself. Father was livid, of course, but then men of his generation are so intolerant.'

Kate shook her head. 'Oh, I don't think so, Lance. It's just that they see their living, and what they've worked for, being threatened by someone they feel has only an academic knowledge of the situation.' She laughed. 'One thing's for sure. This Thornton and our new neighbour should have their heads knocked together.'

She wondered vaguely what the newcomer did for a living. Something in the town, perhaps? A director of one of the many light industries of Norfolk?

Lance touched her cheek. 'Hello, hello!' he said softly. 'The tiger coming out in you?'

She laughed. 'Not as far as your concerned, anyway, Lance.'

'Well, that's nice to know.'

It was odd, Kate thought suddenly. Lance and she had never indulged in these kind of sentimental exchanges before. Was their relationship undergoing a change? She frowned. Love? She was not sure she wanted it. Their previous relationship had been so simple and uncomplicated. But perhaps her father had put new ideas into her head.

It had been an odd sort of day, she thought as she

drove home later. First her encounter with the man Leigh, if that was his name, then her father behaving strangely, the disturbing article in the paper, the unusual morning appearance of Lance's father and finally, the beginnings of a subtle change in Lance's attitude toward her, and hers toward him.

When she entered the house all was quiet and there was a note in her father's writing propped up on the sitting-room mantel. *Gone to the Wherry with Jim. Won't be late, but don't wait up.*

She sighed and went straight up to bed. Perhaps tomorrow would be more normal.

If she had temporarily forgotten that tomorrow was Saturday, she was soon reminded of it the following morning. Saturday, in the world of the boathire business, was the most hectic day of the week. It was the day on which the hired cabin craft as well as the houseboats changed hands. It was a rule that all houseboats should be vacated and craft brought in by ten o'clock. Take-over time was at four, though some holiday-makers began to arrive long before then and strolled or sat around waiting, eager to take possession of their holiday craft. But before they could do this, each houseboat and hire-craft had to be thoroughly cleaned and checked over, the engines and sail equipment overhauled, water tanks filled up, empty or near-empty bottle gas cylinders changed for full ones, clean linen placed in the sleeping cabins, and if the weather had been wet, decks and hulls to be mopped.

The scene was as busy, interesting and fascinating as it was possible to imagine and Kate loved it, largely because very few people complained that they had not enjoyed their holiday. Quite the reverse, even if the weather had been unkind, as the interior of the cabins were so attractive and comfortable.

On a fine morning such as this, the scene was doubly pleasing. Mooring at their quays on Friday night and Saturdays was restricted to boatyard craft only, and there was the continual activity of Martham Boats coming in, the end-of-holiday crews unloading, the cleaning women with their little handcarts loaded with linen and cleaning materials, the engineers dipping tanks, overhauling the engines, fresh arrivals in their gay and nautical slacks and sweaters waiting with patient eagerness to take over their floating, miniature hotel or houseboat.

Clad in jeans and a sweater herself, Kate gave assistance anywhere and everywhere where it was needed, either directing people to the office, handing out lifebelts or portable television sets, helping the big cruisers to come in to moor without knocking paintwork off other craft, showing newcomers over their boat, explaining how to work the shower baths of some of them and in some cases taking first-timers to the Broads on a trial run to initiate them into the rules of the river and the intricacies of handling the craft.

Lunch for Kate and her father was a brief affair of coffee and sandwiches, and Kate was just coming out of the house when across the Broad she saw the new owner of the Grange. Her first reaction was one of anger. How dared he come here when he had been so rude to her? But of course, he probably still did not know who she was. She walked slowly down to the quayside and began helping a family to unload who were late coming in. They had run into difficulties at Berney Arms as a result of ignoring advice given to them and this had delayed them. The cleaning women had gone, which meant she would have to clean out the cruiser herself—something she did not mind in the least, but the sooner the hirers departed the sooner she could get it done.

She was setting a suitcase down when the man from the Grange brought his craft alongside—a brand new motor launch, she noticed. Kate eyed him in silence for a moment, sorely tempted to retaliate by telling him that these were private moorings on private property, but it was really against their code and the public nature of their business. She became conscious that he was eyeing her too, but now he looked different. He was no longer frowning, a fact which made him look much more attractive. Instinctively, she caught hold of his mooring rope and secured it to a post by a deft clove hitch.

'Thank you,' he said in a surprised voice. 'Just finishing your holiday?'

Her eyes widened, then she smiled involuntarily. 'I'm not on holiday. Just helping these folk to unload,' she explained.

He leaped agilely on to the quayside and stood beside her, tall and lean and intensely masculine.

'Do you live in Norfolk, then?' he asked.

'I live here.'

He gave her a swift glance. 'Here? You mean—'

'This is my father's boatyard. We live in the house there—' she gestured toward it, proud of its appearance —the gables, the white paintwork and the extremely attractive thatch of reeds.

'Oh. Oh, I see.'

She glanced at his face, now set into stiff lines. Did the idea displease him? If so, why? She was about to ask him to excuse her and get on with her work when he asked:

'And the Broad? Does your father own that, too?'

'In a way, yes. When Mother and Father first bought the land nobody wanted the Broad because it was overgrown with weeds and unnavigable except for a very narrow channel. Each year, Father had dredging done, the channel widened, until it's as you see it now—a beautiful stretch of clear water people can enjoy.'

He glanced around. 'And moor here to patronize the shop and café—which I presume also belong to your father?'

There was no mistaking his sarcasm or what he was implying by it. Kate felt her anger rising again.

'I don't like your tone, Mr—Leigh. Let me tell you that, but for men like my father, thousands of people might never have had the opportunity of enjoying a scene like this, or of having the wonderful holiday the rivers and Broads provide. My parents love the country and the Broads. They didn't set out to make vast sums of money. The business just grew out of a demand and the shop and café were added to meet a need.'

'I'm sure they were.'

Kate drew a furious breath and was about to tell him that mooring at the quayside was by courtesy of her father and would he please go, but she thought suddenly of something else.

'Well, at least my parents didn't put a barrier up at the entrance of the Broad to keep people out,' she flung at him.

'There was a reason for my barrier,' he answered quietly.

'I'm sure there was,' she flashed back triumphantly.

He gave her a sidelong glance, and she thought she detected a faint glimmer of amusement.

'Let's call it a draw, shall we? And before you order me off may I offer my apologies for yesterday morning. I thought you were—'

'A holiday-maker? I don't think that's any reason at all for being so—'

She broke off, unable to find a word which would not be downright rude. She would have accepted his apology gracefully, if she had thought he was a hundred per cent sincere. Normally she admired people who were big enough to admit a mistake, but she couldn't help feeling that this man didn't really think he *had* been in the wrong.

' I did think you were a holiday-maker at first, yes,' he answered. ' I also thought you were one of those young people with the present-day tendency to ignore barriers, notices, and all rules, who kick against authority of any kind, anywhere, at any time.'

' And how do you know I'm not?'

' On further acquaintance I don't think you are.'

But somehow she was still needled. She felt his tone was patronizing and did not like being regarded by him as being ' one of those young people '—so very much younger than himself.

' Then you could be wrong,' she answered. ' I do object to too many Keep Out notices, Trespassers Will Be Prosecuted, and barriers where they needn't be.'

' Do you deny a person the right to keep intruders off his own property?' he asked.

For a moment she was stuck for a reply to so reasonable a question without conceding the entire argument to him. But after a moment or two of thought, she said,

' No, I wouldn't deny that. But waterways are rather special. Why should you want to keep a nice quiet little waterway like the creek all to yourself? The Major-General did, admittedly, but—'

' But you think I ought to be different.'

' Yes.'

He smiled slightly and inclined his head. ' All the same, I think I shall leave the barrier there—or at least, across the widest part. Local people such as yourself, or others in small boats, are welcome to use it for a quiet row or paddle, but I do want to deter large cruisers, otherwise it will no longer be a nice quiet waterway, will it? In any case there's no point in their going up there. It doesn't lead anywhere except to my house, and I think I have the right to keep my mooring place private.' His lips twitched into a definite, most charming smile and Kate felt something inside her do quite alarming things.

No wonder—if rumour were true—that he was popular with her sex. ' Of course, I shall always be delighted to have a visit from yourself,' he added smoothly.

Kate found herself entirely at a loss for words; not only had his smile quite disarmed her, but he was absolutely right in what he had said about his waterway. Not all of the Broads holiday-makers, particularly some of the ones who hired the large six and eight-berth cruisers loved the countryside enough to care for it. There was always plenty of evidence of vandalism, wilful damage to the river banks and private property, and if he was willing for his waterway to be used by owners of small craft—

She murmured her thanks, increasingly aware of the tremendous attractiveness of the man, and thinking what an awful sight she must look in her soiled jeans and old sweater.

' If—if you'll excuse me, I must get on with my work,' she murmured.

' Right, well, I'll go and take a look at what you've got in your shop.' He turned to go, then hesitated, and added with faint amusement, ' Perhaps when you're through with your chores, you'll join me in your café for a cup of tea.'

He didn't wait to see what her answer was. Kate watched him for a moment as he strode toward the shop with long, easy strides. Now there was a man, she thought suddenly. A real man one could—

She stopped her thoughts short. She had work to do. She had wasted enough time already. But she could not help thinking of their new neighbour from time to time. Perhaps he would come regularly to the boatyard shop. They sold pretty nearly everything in the food line, even meat and poultry in the deep freeze. But it seemed incredible that a man like that was still not either married or engaged. Millie's informant might be wrong.

It did not take long to clean out the cruiser. The

previous hirers had left it pretty tidy, and putting in fresh linen was done in a matter of minutes. By now a good many of the newcomers had loaded their craft with provisions and were already off on their voyage of pleasurable discovery. Her father was at the farther end of the quay showing a family to their houseboat. She strolled over to him.

'Not many more to come now, Father, and all the boats are ready. I think I might go and have a cup of tea.'

He nodded. 'I'm sorry you had the job of cleaning out that cruiser. Why didn't you get one of the women to work overtime?'

'Oh, that's all right. I didn't mind, and the women have got their own families to look after.'

He nodded, gazing across the Broad for a moment in a far-off manner. Then he turned to her.

'By the way, who was that you were talking to about half an hour ago?'

'Oh, that was our new neighbour—the new owner of The Grange. You remember, I told you I'd come across him when I was out early yesterday morning.'

'The one who wasn't very pleased?'

She laughed shortly. 'It was nothing really—and he has apologized. He—thought I was one of those people who disregarded all notices and barriers on principle.'

'Then he judged hastily, didn't he?'

'Yes, but—I really think he's quite nice.'

'Oh? Then I'd better take a look at him myself.'

'He went to the shop. He said he'd go into the café for a cup of tea afterwards.'

'Ah! Well, you run along. I'll come and find you in about five minutes or so.'

Kate popped into the office and ran a comb through her short fair hair. Did this style make her look too plain? she wondered. Perhaps she would look better with it long. A hair-piece with a bandeau might be the answer, but somehow she did not like false hair. She sighed. Her appearance had never particularly worried her before. Now all at once she wanted to look more feminine. But there was no time to change, and it would look odd if she did, so she strolled over to the café, wondering whether Mr Leigh—she didn't know his Christian name—would be there or still looking around the shop.

He was there, talking to Elsie who served behind the counter, and as soon as he saw Kate, he went to a table and pulled out a chair. Almost immediately, Elsie brought a tray with tea and a selection of cakes.

'How lovely,' said Kate. 'A quick cup of tea is usually all I manage on Saturdays.'

'I imagine so. Does your mother help with the business too?'

Kate shook her head and explained, 'We have a daily woman, but she doesn't come in on Saturdays.'

'So you do the housekeeping and help your father in the business? You must mean a great deal to each other.'

Kate smiled. 'No one ever had a better father. But here he comes, so you'll be able to meet him.'

Eric Martham came towards them, and Mr Leigh brought up an extra chair for him, then asked Elsie for another cup and saucer and a plate.

Kate made the introduction. 'Father, this is Mr Leigh who's come to live at the Grange. Mr Leigh—my father.'

'Mr—?' queried the other man holding out his hand. 'I'm afraid your daughter is very bad on names.'

'Martham. Eric Martham,' her father supplied, shaking his hand.

'And mine's Kate. Sorry, I didn't realize you didn't know my name.'

He laughed. 'And you've only got a part of mine. Leigh is my first name. Spelt L, double E. My other name is Thornton.'

CHAPTER II

'Thornton!' Eric Martham's eyes widened alarmingly. 'I hope you're not the man who wrote that article in yesterday's paper.'

Kate stared at Lee, hoping with all her heart that he was not the same man. It was somehow vitally important that her father should like him, and she could not bear it if his ideas about the Broads differed so terribly from their own. Her heart, which had lurched horribly when he had told them his real name, now seemed to stop beating altogether as she waited—hopefully—for him to deny any connection with the article.

He eyed her father steadily, then flicked a glance at herself before answering.

'Yes, I wrote the article,' he said quietly. 'But—'

Eric Martham's face darkened. He took an angry breath and rose slowly to his feet.

'Get out of my café and off my property, do you hear? And don't let me ever see you here again!'

Lee Thornton's face lost its colour, but it returned swiftly as he too stood up.

'I hope you don't mean that, Mr Martham. Surely we—'

'I don't want to hear another word,' Eric Martham said, emphasizing each werd with slow, quiet anger.

Lee's face stiffened. 'Very well. And you, Kate?' he queried.

Kate looked agonizingly from one to the other, then shook her head swiftly and scraped back her chair.

'I—what my father said goes for me too.'

She walked out of the café quickly, wanting nothing more than the privacy of her own room. It was terrible —unbelievable.

In her room she sat at her window gazing out at the Broad, unable to think clearly. All she felt at this moment was that something wonderful had begun to happen only to be completely shattered. She knew a great desire to cry without quite knowing why.

As she sat there, she saw Lee Thornton get in his launch, start his engine and let go his moorings. She watched him cross the Broad, making for the exit, and felt, dramatically perhaps, as if he were going out of her life for ever. She frowned, not quite understanding herself. He was attractive, yes, but why should she feel like this about him? She had plenty of friends, she had Lance.

Lee Thornton's shirt, a brilliant white against the green background of the trees, disappeared from sight altogether. It was difficult to realize that he was the same man who had written that article condemning men like her father, accusing them of ruining the beauty of the Broads out of a greed for money. Yet not so difficult, recalling some of the things he had said only half an hour ago. No wonder her father had been so angry, but if only he hadn't ordered him to leave like that and never come again. Or better still, if only Lee Thornton had never written that article.

Kate moved restlessly about her room. There was not a great deal more work to do now in the boatyard. Only two more lots of hirers still to come and the boats were ready as far as the interior work was concerned. The engineers would attend to the rest, and the girls in the office would be there until four o'clock.

She looked at herself in her long mirror and disliked what she saw—a scrawny, carelessly-dressed, almost slovenly girl who looked more like a seventeen-year-old than the twenty-two-year-old that she was. That was how Lee Thornton must have seen her. No wonder he had looked amused when she tried to argue with him.

He would be annoyed at being ordered off, naturally, but she did not suppose he would give herself another thought. But in any case, she thought, it was time she started looking more her own age and less of a teenager, and she was wondering how to start when a knock came at the door.

'You in there, Katie?'

'Yes, Father. Come in.'

He opened the door. 'I wondered where you'd got to, you shot off so quickly.' He gave her a keen glance. 'I don't know how that fellow had the nerve to show up here.'

'Did you—really mean that, Father, about his not coming here again?'

'I certainly did. Why? Don't you agree?'

'Well, he'd probably have done a good bit of his shopping here. For food and so on, I mean.'

'We can do without his patronage. He isn't likely to come near the place again, anyhow. If he does—'

'What then? You can't get a gun to him every time you see him, can you?'

'Don't try me,' he said darkly. He gave her another keen look. 'You ranged yourself on my side and I appreciate that. But you didn't look altogether happy about it. This—fellow surely doesn't mean anything to you? Not on a couple of meetings?'

'Of course not, Father,' she said swiftly, moving to the window again. 'But after he apologized for the other morning, I thought he did seem rather nice, that's all.'

'Rather nice! He'd take the bread out of our mouths.'

Kate frowned. 'He was only generalizing in that article. Perhaps if you'd got to know each other a little—'

Eric Martham gave a derisive grunt. 'His views were

set down pretty plainly. And he didn't look to me like a man who'd say things he doesn't mean. No, Kate, I meant what I said. I don't want him near the place and the best thing you can do is forget him. That won't be difficult, will it? In any case, he's too old for you by far.'

Kate laughed. 'Good heavens, Father, you talk as though I've fallen head over heels in love at first sight— or second, because I certainly didn't at first.' She shrugged. 'I just think it's a pity he turned out to be *that* man. It would have been nice to have had a friendly neighbour.'

Her father put a hand on her shoulder. 'As long as you're happy, that's all I want, Kate.' He went to the door. 'Have you finished for the day?'

'I just thought I'd change. I look such a scarecrow.'

'You never look that, my dear. But you've done enough for one day out there, anyhow. I'll attend to anything else. You do as you please. You going out tonight?'

'Only to the Wherry as usual.'

It was the custom with the boathire fraternity in the area to drift along to the Wherry on Saturdays when they had finished settling in their holiday people. Some might be early, but often they were late, particularly in the height of summer, and most of Kate's crowd gathered there for a drink of some kind and talk.

Her father nodded. 'Well, we can eat whenever you like. I'm easy. I might drop in myself later.'

Kate sighed as he went out and closed the door behind him. Life was very difficult all at once. She had tried to reassure her father about Lee Thornton. She hadn't fallen in love with him, of course. You simply did not fall in love as quickly as all that. All the same, there was something about him, even when they had been arguing, which attracted her enormously. He was quite

35

the most interesting, intriguing, dynamic man she had ever met.

She caught herself up with an angry impatient gesture. How could she be thinking this way of a man whose ideas were so opposed to her father's? In fact, if he was sincere about everything he had said in his article she must surely despise him.

The thought made her curl up inside. Perhaps he despised her, too. She sighed and tried to put these depressing and useless speculations out of her mind. As her father said, she would forget Lee Thornton. She had a bath, then put on another pair of slacks and a sweater, discarding any faint notion of wearing a dress. All of the crowd at the Wherry would be so attired. If she turned up wearing anything else she would never stop answering questions.

She cooked a meal for her father and herself, then when she had cleared away, went without much heart to the Wherry.

It was a place which always intrigued her, in spite of knowing it so well. The saloon was fashioned in the shape of a clinker-built hull and the copper fastenings polished until they glinted like gold. Behind the bar, port and starboard lights cast a red and green light over the room. The other lighting came from masthead and not-under-command lights set in a burnished copper. A teak steering wheel completed the effect while around the room at intervals were hung lifebelts. The windows were in the shape of portholes with their dead-light covers and on the walls were also charts and ancient maps.

Lance was already there. Obviously looking out for her, he hailed her as soon as she walked in. He elbowed his way through the crowd in their slacks and brightly coloured sweaters or casual jackets, and put an arm around her shoulders.

' I've been saving a seat for you. This place gets more

popular week by week. I'm glad Father decided to put a manager in charge. It lets me off.'

He pushed a way back to a table at which were seated Tony Sheldrake, Lindy Brown and David Lines.

Lance pushed a long drink in front of her. ' Millie was here until a few minutes ago. She's talking to a man at the bar—I rather think it's that new neighbour of yours—the lady-killer.'

Something inside Kate contracted sharply. She glanced across at the hull-shaped bar. Millie was talking avidly, putting on all her charm as only Millie could, and Lee Thornton was smiling, obviously enjoying the conversation.

' Looks as though she's making a hit,' said David.

Kate turned away and picked up her glass without comment. ' Had a busy day, Lance?' she asked.

' The usual.' He searched her face. ' You look as though yours might have been a bit harrowing. Has it?'

She shrugged. ' Well, you know. This and that. One lot got themselves into difficulties and didn't get in until about two when the cleaners had gone home.'

She didn't want to relate the scene between Lee Thornton and her father to all of them. To Lance perhaps, later.

' Tough luck,' sympathized Lance.

Lindy was looking toward Millie and Lee with great interest. ' Millie said she'd bring him over. I wonder if he'll come? They're looking this way now.'

' I think we're all being pointed out,' said David.

Kate hoped Millie wouldn't bring him over. After what had happened that afternoon it would be most embarrassing. She would come face to face with him somewhere at some time in the future, she supposed, but by that time the incident would no longer be quite so fresh.

Lance yawned. ' I don't know why all this terrific interest in a new face.'

'I agree,' Tony put in. 'Anyone would think there was a shortage of the male of the species instead of *vice versa*.'

Lindy winked at Kate. 'Well, I think he looks fabulous. Look at that profile—the strong jaw, the manly chin.'

'Thanks a lot,' David said, sarcastically fingering his own chin.

Lindy gave an excited squeak. 'He's coming over. Katie, how do I look?'

'Fine,' Kate told her. Lindy was only saying these things to tease David. She was actually in love with him, and though they were not exactly engaged, everyone expected they would eventually marry. She held her breath and waited for Millie and Lee to join them, but much to the disappointment of Lindy, Millie was alone when she reached their table.

'Well?' Lindy demanded. 'I thought you were—'

Millie shook her head and sat down. 'He's terrific. He's been telling me all about himself. He's a consultant marine engineer and his name's Thornton, not Leigh. Lee Thornton.'

'Lee Thornton!' came from Lance. 'Why, that's the name of the man who wrote that article condemning any further development on the Broads and recommending a limit on the number of holiday cruisers and houseboats. Well, what do you think about that, Kate?'

She sighed. 'I know. He came to our place this afternoon and I found out then.'

'But why on earth didn't you tell me? No wonder you were looking so shattered. He had a nerve, I must say.'

'Oh, you boathire people. You take this Broads controversy too seriously,' said Millie.

'So would you if your living depended on boathire,' Lance told her. 'Your father's in boatbuilding for export, so he isn't quite so concerned about the Broads.'

'Thornton is only one voice anyway, Lance,' David offered.

'Of course, it depends how much more developing you want to do. Holiday hire business is getting to be a real headache, anyway,' Tony said. 'My father is talking about selling out and getting out.'

'Well, mine isn't. He wants to develop some riverside property we have on the south side—on the Yare.'

But neither Lindy nor Millie wanted to talk shop. 'Why didn't you bring him over?' Lindy asked.

'I did ask him, but he said he had some business to attend to,' answered Millie ruefully.

'I bet he has,' Lance muttered.

'He said he'd already met Kate, but would look forward to meeting the rest of you some other time.'

'That's very kind of him,' Lance said sarcastically. 'Well, I for one don't want to meet *him*.'

'Oh, come on now, Lance,' Millie protested. 'You can't bring business into your social life all the time.'

'I can when it comes to a man with his ideas. Anyway, he doesn't look as if he'd fit in with our social set.'

'Not fit in? What on earth do you mean?'

'He looks at least ten years older than we are, for one thing.'

Millie's chin went up. 'I think that's part of his— well, his charm.'

'His charm, my foot!' Lance pushed back his chair. 'Come on, Kate, let's go for a walk or something. I've had enough of this conversation.'

Kate rose. 'So have I.'

They went out. Kate had never felt so ragged in her life. Lance, too, was unusually put out.

'Millie really gets my goat at times,' he muttered. 'All that talk about charm and Thornton being " terrific " !'

'I know how you feel,' sympathized Kate. 'He certainly seems to be a disturbing influence one way and another.'

'You can say that again,' Lance said gloomily.

Kate was too occupied in coping with her own ragged feelings to wonder why Lance should allow Millie to upset him so much. She suggested a walk and they climbed the little hill towards the church.

'This scheme of Father's—to develop those mooring plots on the Yare,' Lance said after a while. 'Do you know what he has in mind?'

'Well, he did say he was doing it for you, Lance.'

'Yes, he wants me to run my own place. Very decent of him. He seems to think I shall be getting married soon—or ought to be.'

Kate laughed briefly. 'That's odd. Father thinks the same with regard to me.'

Lance took her hand and led her to a five-barred gate. 'What do you think, Katie? Shall we?'

'Get married, you mean? I don't know. I don't think I want to yet.'

Lance frowned and slid an arm across her shoulders. 'I think I do. Will you, Kate—if Father gets planning permission for the new place?'

Kate felt troubled. She was not really in love with Lance. Suddenly she knew that.

He pulled her towards him and kissed her. Kate heard a car roar up the hill and as the vehicle passed them, Lance gave a quick look.

'Hm!' he grunted derisively. 'That was the charming Lee Thornton—and he had a woman with him. A very attractive-looking one, too. I wonder what Millie would say to that?'

Kate sighed. 'Lance, I think I'll get along home, if you don't mind. I could do with an early night.'

He gave her a reproachful look. 'You didn't answer

40

my question.'

'Lance, I've told you. I don't want to get married yet. And I don't think we've got that kind of feeling for each other.'

'I have for you.'

'No, Lance, I'm quite sure you haven't. Maybe you're feeling restless or something. So many of us are. It must be the spring. Come on, let's go.'

As they walked back towards the Wherry Kate wondered who the woman had been with Lee Thornton. It seemed he was living up to his reputation.

Sunday was counted as one of Kate's days off. Often, she and Lance did something together, but before they had said goodnight he made no mention of seeing her, and Kate was glad. After a late breakfast, she filled a flask with coffee and pushed off in the half-decker with the hope of a peaceful sail. The weather was holding good, and there was a fair breeze. As she passed the entrance to the inlet leading to the Grange, she glanced in that direction and noticed that the barrier was still there. He had said he would be delighted to see her, but that was before he had met her father. She couldn't help wishing her father had not been quite so drastic. But it was difficult to reconcile people of such different views, and she had had no option but to stand by her father.

The *Aerial* barely moved along the cut leading to the open river on account of the trees which lined the bank. They were beautiful trees, but they certainly served to blanket off the wind for sailing. Someone had once suggested to her father that they might be felled for that reason, but he had refused. He loved trees. He loved the country. That was what made it so ridiculous when people like her father and Lee Thornton were at logger-heads in spite of the fact that at heart they both loved the same things.

She turned into the main river. Now the wind filled out the lug sail and sent the half-decker gliding smoothly along the water. But soon the river took on a long curve. The wind came more astern and the boom pulled strongly on the main sheet. Kate let more of the rope slide out of her hold. As the sail swung out, the boat picked up speed, and Kate thrilled to the sound of the bow ripple, like water gurgling over stones.

A little way ahead Kate knew there was a sharp double bend with heavy tree growth and an old windmill, both of which either cut the wind off entirely or made its direction unpredictable. She rounded the first bend easily, then had to haul in the main sheet and execute a tack. She was running free when she saw the stern of a launch half hidden in a clump of bushes. She put her tiller over and thought she would clear the launch easily, but at the crucial moment the breeze failed completely. The boat lost way and failed to respond to the rudder no matter how frantically she tried to steer. Inexorably the boat drifted straight into the launch. The bump when it came was only a light one, but she heard the clatter of falling crockery, and as a man jumped to his feet with a muttered exclamation she looked straight into the eyes of Lee Thornton.

He glared. 'You again? What's gone wrong with your sense of direction this time?'

His tone angered her so much, her apology died in her throat.

'There's no need to be rude,' she flashed back. 'I couldn't help it. I lost wind suddenly because of all these trees, and anybody knows you can't steer if you haven't enough way.'

He didn't answer, but his expression relaxed a little. He picked up a beaker from the floor of his launch and held it upside down.

'That was my coffee.'

Her anger died. 'I'm sorry—truly. I have some. Will you—share it with me?'

He eyed her dubiously for a second, then said: 'Thank you. But perhaps it would be better if we sat on the bank.'

He sprang ashore and made her boat secure, then spread out his coat for her to sit on. Kate leaned over and put her flask on the grass, then followed with a light jump.

She poured out the coffee, feeling a nagging disloyalty to her father, yet at the same time an acute embarrassment on her own behalf. There was a rather long, and to Kate, uncomfortable silence, then Lee Thornton said conversationally:

'That's a very handy boat you have there.'

'Yes, it is.'

They entered into a discussion about boats and sailing, then there was another silence, until at last Kate felt bound to speak about what was on her mind.

'Mr Thornton, I—I'm really awfully sorry about what happened yesterday afternoon. My—father isn't usually like that. It—it was that article of yours, you see.'

'So I gathered,' he said drily. Then he pointed out: 'I did try to reconcile our differences, and then you, too—'

'Yes, I know. But what else could I do? I—I'm all my father has.'

'Your loyalty does you credit, of course. But would he mind your talking to me like this—away from the boatyard?'

'I don't know. And it's all so—so difficult. I mean, so silly. I'm sure you and Father *do* have a lot in common.'

'Such as?' he queried with underlying sarcasm.

She gave him an angry look. 'If you're going to be

43

unpleasant—' She made a move to get up, but he restrained her.

'Finish your coffee. I daresay we have got things in common, and I can well understand his anger in view of the things I said in my article about men in the boat-hire business.'

'The thing is, I can see both points of view and I don't see why—'

'Obviously, not everyone is so tolerant.'

'Perhaps in father's place, I wouldn't be.'

'Perhaps not,' he agreed. 'But even as his daughter it's to your advantage if his business is successful. And —er—you have—special friends in the business too, haven't you?'

She coloured slightly, remembering that he must have seen her in Lance's arms yesterday evening.

'Yes, but that doesn't make me disagree with everything in your article.'

He gave her a long look. 'What things did you agree with?'

She gazed reflectively across the water. 'Well, that the natural beauty of the rivers and Broads should be preserved, of course.' She smiled suddenly. 'And I thought the bit about "strings of fairy lights from one landscaped tree, etc. to another," was very funny.'

His answering smile was a little grim. 'It wasn't really meant to be funny.'

'Sarcastic?'

'A warning. That's what it could come to if some people have their way. Did you agree that there should be a restriction on the number of motor cruisers on the Broads as a whole?'

She frowned. 'Well, I wouldn't go so far as to say that, but—'

'There can't be any buts, otherwise it's just paying lip service to say you want to preserve the beauty and natural amenities of the rivers and Broads system.'

She coloured angrily. 'You really are intolerant, aren't you?'

'You have to know where you stand and stick to it. You see? When a thing really touches your pocket, such as whether to restrict the number of motor cruisers, then you balk.'

'That's not fair!'

'So you don't think saturation point has been reached yet?'

She frowned. 'But it's ridiculous to say it has. There are plenty of nice quiet places on the Broads. On the south side you can sail for miles and hardly see one cruiser.'

He gave a derisive laugh. 'That's poppycock. And I daresay there are *some* quiet places left. That's the whole idea, the whole attraction of the Norfolk Broads —that people can get away from crowds. But it won't stay that way if those who care don't watch out. There's plenty of room in the sky, but that doesn't mean we want to fill it with gliders, kites, jet planes and the like.'

'There's no need to exaggerate,' she said hotly, stung by his sarcasm in which he appeared to specialize.

'You think I'm exaggerating? That shows how little you really understand the situation.'

Kate got to her feet angrily. 'I suppose you think you're the only person in the world who does understand? I can see it's no use whatever trying to reason with you.'

She screwed the top of her flask on swiftly and scrambled aboard the half-decker, both angry and disappointed.

He stood on the bank and looked down at her, smiling faintly. 'Thanks for the coffee,' he said. 'But I'm sorry you have to go so soon.'

More sarcasm. She thought it more likely that he

was glad to see the back of her. He let go her moorings for her and gave her a push off, sending her skimming across to the opposite bank in a tack. In waving her thanks, her anger died, leaving only her sense of acute disappointment that their sharing of coffee and conversation had ended in argument. They were destined, it seemed, to quarrel.

She tacked from one bank to the other, gaining a little more each time, until a bend in the river gave her a beam wind and took her out of sight of Lee Thornton. She did not put him out of her mind, however. The wind filled her sail and sent her skimming along, her bow wave making delicious lapping noises, but she was thinking how nice it would have been if they could have been real friends, even considering the difference in their ages. She had a feeling that he was a man to whom one could always turn, rely upon, trust. If only he had never written that article, if only he and her father did not hold such extreme views.

The next time the half-decker came head into wind Kate turned about and made for home again. She kept a sharp look-out for Lee, but did not see him and concluded that he had returned home, too. She did not mention her encounter with him to her father. There was no point in angering him further.

The following day Kate was lending a hand in the quayside store when a most attractive woman entered whose face was vaguely familiar, yet Kate knew she had never seen her before. It was difficult to tell her age. She was not young. There was a maturity about her and a quiet charm, but she was not middle-aged either. She was slender, her hair was dark and of a medium length and she was wearing a sleeveless shirt-waister dress which suited her perfectly. *The sort of woman Lee Thornton might admire.* The thought flashed through Kate's mind unbidden. The woman bought so many items of

46

both grocery and greengrocery that Kate insisted on packing them into two cartons for her.

'I'll get one of the men to carry them down to your boat,' she offered. 'What's the name of it?'

'It's a small private launch. The blue one.'

'Blue? Are you local? If so, perhaps we can deliver them for you.'

The woman smiled and shook her head. 'It's quite all right. My son will take care of them at the other end. Later, perhaps when you're not so busy, I'll be glad to have them delivered.'

Kate called to one of the workmen to carry the cartons to the launch, then strolled down to the quayside with her customer and was about to ask where she lived, when the woman asked, surprisingly:

'Are you Kate?'

'Why, yes.'

The woman turned and put out a hand. 'I'm Jane Thornton. Please—I do hope we can be friends.'

Kate drew in her breath swiftly and held out her own hand, a smile of pleasure lighting her face.

'You mean—'

'I'm Lee's mother. He's told me about you.'

'Lee's mother? Oh, but you can't be.'

'Why not?'

'You're so—young-looking and—and attractive.'

Jane Thornton threw back her head and laughed. 'And you're not finding Lee attractive? He wouldn't be very flattered.'

'Oh, but I didn't mean—'

Jane patted her shoulder. 'Don't worry. I believe there are one or two things you and he don't quite see eye to eye about, but—'

'Did he tell you that?'

'Well, in a way. We're—very close, Lee and I, as I expect you and your father are. Lee has no father, and

47

I understand you have no mother.'

' I can't even remember her, but Father still keeps her photograph on his dressing table.'

Jane Thornton's expression softened. 'That's wonderful. Really wonderful. Lee can just remember his father. He was killed towards the end of the war.'

' And you never married again?'

Jane shook her head. ' It really doesn't seem all that long ago, and once you've known great love—well, another is very difficult to find, even if you're looking. And I—haven't been looking.'

' I understand.'

For a few moments neither spoke. Kate felt an affinity with the older woman she could not have described, and after a second or two Jane turned to her, a soft half-smile on her face as if her thoughts which had been far away and long ago still lingered.

' I'm sure you do, my dear. I think you're a very sweet and understanding person.'

Kate smiled, then a look of distress creased her features.

' I—suppose Mr Thornton told you—'

' Lee, please. He would prefer it, I'm sure, and so do I.'

Kate nodded. ' Did he—did Lee tell you about Father —the other day?'

' Ordering him off the premises? Yes, he did mention it.'

' And that I—'

' That, too. It was rather silly of him to put you in the position of having to—verbally support your father. I say that because I think it has made difficulties for you. Is your father a very strict or stern kind of man?'

' Why, no, not really. He was already angry about that article, then meeting its author like that—it angered him even more. He's normally a very friendly and

48

sociable person.'

Jane Thornton sighed and shook her head. 'It's all a very great pity, and Lee can be stubborn at times. But, my dear, all that business needn't stop you and me from becoming friends, I'm sure. And who knows one day we might succeed in bringing the two of them together.'

'If extreme views can be reconciled,' Kate said doubtfully.

'Are they so very extreme?'

Kate frowned thoughtfully at the query. 'I suppose not when it comes to fundamentals—at least, not about everything. But they're certainly both very forthright.' She smiled ruefully. 'I'm afraid Lee and I got to disagreeing with each other yesterday morning.'

Jane smiled. 'That isn't really very surprising. But I must go now, Kate. I shall be coming along fairly often for shopping, so I'll see you again soon. Perhaps one of these days I shall come across your father. But don't introduce us. Better let us get to know each other first. Then maybe one day you could come and have tea with me.'

Kate held the launch steady while Jane stepped down, then waved as the launch chugged in the direction of the Broad exit. She had rarely, if ever, met a woman she liked so much.

It was difficult, the next time she was talking to her father, not to tell him about her. Only the thought that he might immediately be prejudiced against her because of Lee helped her to keep silent.

It was only later, in her room, when her father had gone to the Wherry to see Jim Faulkner, that she asked herself why it meant so much to her that her father should like Mrs Thornton and that he and Lee should one day become friends. She thought about it for a long time. She thought about Lee, his views about the Broads

49

and the future of Broadland, and as himself, as a man. She sat at her window and looked out on to the Broad and remembered, not so much the morning of their first encounter, but the afternoon when they had stood and talked together at the quayside, the way he had looked, his brown arms against his white shirt, the lines of his jaw, the smooth skin under his eyes, the way he spoke, his smile.

She couldn't possibly marry Lance. Already, she was in love with Lee Thornton.

CHAPTER III

On acknowledging that she had fallen in love with Lee
Thornton, Kate was more appalled than happy. Nothing
could ever come of it. Neither Lee nor her father would
be willing to change their views, Lee was forbidden to
set foot even on the staithe, and most important of all,
Lee himself regarded her, at best, with the tolerant
amusement of adult toward adolescent. At worst, he
thought her a person whose views were influenced only
by money. The best thing she could do was put him
right out of her mind.

Suddenly the whole house seemed to shake as the front
door slammed shut. Kate rose to her feet swiftly, her
stomach muscles tightening. It could only be her father,
but he rarely slammed a door in that fashion. She went
to the top of the stairs.

'Father—?' There was no reply. Kate descended a
few stairs then called out again. 'Is that you, Father?'

There was a further pause, then: 'Yes, it's me, Kate,'
came the answer in an angry voice.

She ran down the rest of the stairs and found him
standing looking out of the sitting room window, his
hands thrust deep in his pockets, his shoulders hunched,
his body tense.

'Father, what's the matter?'

He gave a slight start, then turned, his face lined with
anger.

'That—that Thornton fellow. I'd like to wring his
neck!'

Kate's heart contracted violently. 'Why? What—'

'Jim has been refused planning permission for that
proposed development of his on the Yare.'

'But—but, Father, you can't blame L—Mr Thornton

for that, surely? He was only expressing an opinion in his article.'

Eric Martham drew an angry breath. 'I know what I'm talking about, Kate. He's a consultant, isn't he? Well, he was consulted on this occasion and you can guess what his advice was. There was a lot of blabbing about "the wild beauty of the marshes" and "preservation", of "calling a halt", of "checking commercialization". Some of these bods haven't the slightest idea what they're talking about.'

Kate hated to hear her father talk like this. If she did not know him well, she would think he cared very little for preserving beauty, but quite a lot for making money —which was not true at all.

'Father, I don't understand. Why are you so angry about this? I know Mr Faulkner's a friend of yours, but—'

'But what?' he came back swiftly. 'Aren't we supposed to care about our friends and their difficulties?'

'Yes, of course.' It was the only possible answer, though Kate was still extremely puzzled. Jim Faulkner was not destitute, he already had a perfectly good business, and it was not a matter of life or death that Lance should have a business of his own. She gave an inaudible sigh.

'Would you like a cup of tea, Father, or some coffee?'

'Coffee, please, Katie, and make it good and strong.'

Kate put an extra spoonful of coffee in the percolator, and while it was brewing, made a ham sandwich. It was odd that for years one's life could go along on the most even keel, then all at once things began to happen and life was never the same again. Not only had Lee come into her life, but there was something she could not understand happening to her father, some difference in him.

'What is Mr Faulkner going to do, then?' she asked

52

to bridge the silence into which her father lapsed as he drank his coffee and ate a sandwich. ' Is he going to appeal?'

' I don't think so. At least, I advised him not to. The way things are at the moment—with people like Thornton shouting their heads off, I don't think there's much of a hope. The world is so full of long-haired idealists—'

' Mr Thornton hasn't got long hair.'

' Don't quibble, Kate. You know perfectly well what I mean. This part of the country is thick with country squires and faded aristocracy, writers and artists and the like. They think they know it all, and they assume that nobody loves nature or cares about the countryside except themselves. Men like Jim Faulkner and myself are well beyond the pale. You'd think it was a crime to earn a living and want to pass on a good life to your children.'

He paused, then brought himself back to the point. ' No, no, it's not a bit of use Jim appealing. Naturally, he has sunk good money into those mooring plots. He thought he was looking into the future, of course. But to my mind, he was just that little bit too late. There's a boom time in everything, and I'm beginning to think that the boom in the Broads holiday business has come and gone. Personally, I still think there's room for still more expansion, and a few more amenities on the Yare and Waveney would have been a jolly good thing all round, in spite of what Thornton or anybody says.'

' What do you think Mr Faulkner ought to do?' Kate asked, thinking it might do her father good to get everything off his chest, rather than bottle it up in silence.

' Cut his losses, as all business men have to do at times. To begin with, he's asking much too high a price for those mooring plots. He was banking on the fact that with the increased interest in boating—which has been

53

phenomenal in recent years—the shortage of mooring plots, and the high wages of some workers, he would make some money on capital investment rather than putting labour into a new business. But it isn't working out that way. And of course, in his crystal ball he could see the marshes south of Yarmouth being developed and therefore more picturesque and inviting. What looks like " wild beauty " to some people appears just bleak and uninteresting to others. Now it looks as if the kybosh has been put on everything. The only thing he can do now is bring down the price of his mooring plots—he'll have to, because he hasn't even been able to get planning permission for small cedar chalets that people could keep a couple of deck chairs and the like in—and look out for a small existing business on the north side and develop that—or rather, let Lance develop it.'

It still seemed to Kate a lot of unnecessary worry and effort. ' But does Lance really want a business of his own? '

Her father shot her a keen look. ' Of course he does. You should know that. It'll be better for him, anyway. Jim's still comparatively young himself. He'll live for a good many more years yet, and he has another son besides Lance, as well you know.'

' But if Lance went into partnership with his father, he could save enough money to buy his own business some time if he wanted to, without his father doing it for him. There's no hurry, surely? '

Eric Martham sighed. ' Well, Jim thinks differently, and so do I. There are some aspects of parenthood you can't possibly understand, Kate, fatherhood in particular.'

Kate laughed. ' Well, I can't be expected to know what it's like to be a father, can I? I know how a daughter feels, though, and I also know that I've got

54

the best father in the world,' she added impulsively.

She was rewarded by a softening of his expression and a fond look.

' You're a great comfort to me, Kate—but a bit of a responsibility, too. I only wish—'

' Mother?' she prompted gently.

He sighed again and nodded. ' With the best will in the world I can't be both to you, not really.'

' But, Father, you have been,' she insisted. ' It's my turn now to worry about you.'

He frowned and his look alerted. ' Me?'

' Yes, Father. But " with the best will in the world ", I can't take Mother's place.' He closed his eyes momentarily and she knew she had probed deep. ' Father, I know how you felt about Mother—how you still feel—but have you ever thought of marrying again?'

With a half groan he bent his head in his hands. ' Oh, Kate, Kate, if only it were that easy! I don't think the woman is born who could match up to your mother. She would have to be someone very very special indeed.' He raised his head. ' In any case, I wouldn't ever marry again until you were settled down in your own place.'

She tried to argue with him, but he shook his head vigorously. ' No, Kate, I don't want to talk any more about it except this. I would feel happier if you'd make up your mind to marry Lance. He's a decent boy with good prospects and I want to make sure you're going to be happy.'

Kate got to her feet swiftly and began to clear away the coffee cups. How could she possibly be happy with anyone now except Lee?

On Tuesday evening Lance telephoned. ' What would you like to do tomorrow, Kate?' he asked.

Wednesday was their ' day off '—one which they usually spent together or with another couple of friends. Kate thought momentarily that she would rather have

55

gone off somewhere on her own, but she couldn't blame Lance for taking it for granted they would spend it together, and alone she would only think too much about Lee.

'I—don't much mind what we do,' she answered, then made the suggestion: 'A day on the river?'

'Er—no, Kate, if you don't mind. I think I see enough of the river. I'd like to take a run out somewhere, have a nice lunch, then come back and change and have a night out—a film or a spot of dancing.'

'Sounds fine.'

She knew Lance did not share her passion for sailing and so a day on the river would have meant a motor launch, in any case. So he arranged to call for her about eleven.

'That'll give us both a nice sleep in, if we want to,' he said.

Kate often did sleep in on Wednesdays, and on occasions her father even took her breakfast up to her, but this morning she woke early and discovered that, already Lee was on her mind. She padded to the window and saw it was a similar morning to the one on which she had first met him. Like herself, he had been up early that morning. Was he an habitually early riser?

Without stopping to think she washed her hands and face and brushed her teeth, then pulled on a pair of slacks and her nicest sweater and ran downstairs. This time she pushed out a small rowing boat, and with a thrill of excitement sent the boat scudding through the mist toward the exit of the Broad. The entrance to Lee's creek still had a barrier across its widest part, but she noticed he had left a small gap at the side just big enough for a small craft, and had cleared away all the weeds and other growth.

She passed into the creek feeling like a child who is going to be crowned Queen of the May. Forgotten was their argument of Sunday morning, or the fact that—if her father's surmise was correct—he had been instrumental in Lance's father's being refused planning permission for his development scheme. All she knew was, she might possibly see Lee. This time she glanced constantly over her shoulder and kept her ears open for the slightest sound of either oars or an engine. She did not want to collide with him again.

Then, just as she was beginning to think she was not going to see him after all, she detected a slight movement in a reed bed in the bank. She gave a hearty pull on the oars, then let the boat move in its own way for the next few feet, coming up to where she had seen the movement.

It was Lee, sitting motionless watching something. Kate held her breath, hoping she would not disturb whatever it was and so anger him. Then she saw it herself. A heron, as slim and statuesque as a piece of grey stone a few feet away. It was difficult to believe that it was not indeed a stone statue one sees occasionally as ornaments in gardens. Kate shipped her oars as quietly as she could and grasped an overhanging branch to bring the boat to a standstill. Lee turned his head and exchanged a glance with her, but neither spoke. The heron, two feet tall—three altogether—was still motionless, its large pointed bill stretched upwards, its head tucked well into its shoulders—a rare enough sight even in this environment. Then, whether tired of waiting for its prey or disliking the presence of humans, it suddenly rose into the air, neck withdrawn, feet outstretched and its great wings moving slowly. Both Lee and Kate watched it out of sight, then Lee turned and spoke.

' Hello. Do you make a habit of getting up at crack of dawn?'

Her heart gave one or two rapid beats. She looked at his lean, clear features and was glad that she loved him.

She smiled.

' It's a habit I'm rapidly acquiring. But I hope I haven't disturbed your bird-watching.'

He shook his head. ' I wasn't really bird-watching—except the heron, and he was here before I was. I'm afraid we're probably both responsible for disturbing his prey and doing him out of his breakfast.'

' I suppose so. He lives on water-rats and frogs, doesn't he?'

' And fish. Still, I daresay he'll find plenty more.' He was silent for a moment, then suddenly he shot her a keen glance mingled with a hint of ironical amusement. ' I suppose my name is mud now.'

She gave him a puzzled look. ' I don't know what you mean.'

' Surely you do. Jim Faulkner's son is a friend of yours, isn't he? More than a friend, I should say.'

Understanding dawned. ' Oh, you're referring to Mr Faulkner being refused planning permission for his project on the Yare?'

' That's right,' he said, still eyeing her intently.

His scrutiny was beginning to unnerve her. She moved restlessly in the small boat and hardly aware of what she was doing, picked up her oars.

' You—could hardly expect me to be pleased, could you?' she said jerkily. ' Did you do it purposely?'

' Did I do what purposely?'

' Well, did you know who was involved?'

' Not at the time. I learned afterwards.'

' Would it have made any difference?'

' No, I'm afraid it wouldn't. My advice would have still been the same.'

Kate felt as hurt as if she had been refused a personal favour by him.

' You don't care how much you hurt people, do you?' she was stung to come back.

He raised his eyebrows. 'That's a very odd accusation. Whom have I supposed to have hurt? Surely not Jim Faulkner. He already has a thriving business.'

She inhaled deeply. 'He—wanted the new development for Lance.'

'Oh, I see,' he said slowly.

'No, you don't. You don't see at all.'

Afraid of giving herself away, she dipped an oar into the water and spun the dinghy around, only missing his craft by a bare inch.

'You going—so soon?' he called out in a sarcastic tone.

She did not answer. She felt confused, hurt and angry. At this moment she felt she hated him. Not wanting to have her face turned towards him, she rowed in reverse, looking the way she was going, and soon reached the barrier to the inlet. Why was it that every time they met they ended up by quarrelling, or at any rate, by him becoming sarcastic and herself angry? And she had been so hoping to see him this morning! No wonder she was in such a state of confusion.

She rowed across the Broad and crept into the house with a heavy heart. She made the usual preparations for breakfast, continuing to think miserably of Lee. It would have been better if she had never met him. She felt she would never be the same again.

When her father came downstairs he looked at her in surprise.

'You're up early on your day off, aren't you?'

She drew in a swift breath. 'Heavens, I forgot all about it.'

Eric Martham added amusement to his look. 'Lord, you're in a bad way. Are you all right?'

She forced a brief laugh. 'It's the weather. I don't seem to sleep so late these mornings.'

'Mm. Are you seeing Lance today?'

59

She told him she was and there was no doubt that her answer pleased him, but Kate felt troubled.

Lance called at eleven and Kate served coffee in a small room overlooking the garden and out of sight of the Broad. Kate couldn't help noticing that he too, looked rather out of sorts.

' I expect yesterday's business has upset both you and your father,' she remarked.

He nodded gloomily. ' Father's so set on it—for my sake—and it's making me feel guilty. I can neither whip up the same feelings against certain people that he has nor the enthusiasm for the project that he would like me to have. I'm convinced that the peak of development on the Broads has been reached. Any more would destroy the very thing which has made Broads holidays afloat so popular! The peace and seclusion, the freedom. With the publication of the Report there's too much feeling against more development for there to be any more plans passed. I'm sure of it. Father's left it too late. He's made a bad mistake in buying that land, but he won't admit it. Just because there appear to be more and more people with more and more money to throw around, he seemed to think those mooring plots of his would sell like hot cakes. I told him at the time he was asking too much for them, but he wouldn't listen.'

' Perhaps he'll put the price down now,' Kate suggested.

' Perhaps, but whatever he does it will be a waste of time appealing against the decision of the planning authority.'

' Father is of that opinion, too.'

' I know, and I hope to goodness my father listens to him.'

' Maybe Father'll persuade him to buy up a small existing boathire business on this side. It might be possible to develop an existing business, but not start a new

60

one. Anyway, it's chalets and restaurants and the like that the planners are against.'

Lance frowned thoughtfully. 'It's awfully difficult to know where to draw the line, particularly when you're personally involved. I mean, your father was doing a service when he built your milk bar and shop, and holiday-makers as well as residents like the Wherry, but I think enough's enough. If there are too many amenities like that the Broads will begin to attract the wrong kind of people, those who don't so much like the country as a gay old time.'

'I'm sure your father doesn't want that,' Kate protested mildly.

'I agree, he doesn't. But he's part of it—a contributor. Or would be. He's so anxious to see me established. I don't know why. If only he'd let me stand on my own feet. I think that's the biggest mistake parents are making these days. They want to do too much for us. But for one thing, we haven't got the same ambitions that they had. It's a throwback, I suppose. The poor of their day—their *young* days, saw the rich with their fine houses and big cars and they worked and struggled like mad to have the same. At the same time they resented having to work so hard for what they wanted. They don't want us to have the same struggles, so they bend over backwards to make life easy for us. Either that, or it's a sort of fever that gets into them—making money, almost like the old gold rushes.'

Kate smiled sympathetically. 'There's a lot in what you say, Lance, and I'm sure it's true in a good many instances. But people differ so much. Some fellows of your age are just as ambitious as their fathers.'

He sighed. 'I suppose so, and I think it maddens Father that I'm not. I'm willing to put in a fair day's work, and I want a good life, but I don't particularly want a large house, an expensive car or money in the bank.'

Kate laughed. ' I suspect that half the people with large houses and expensive cars haven't *got* money in the bank. But Father always says that the young aren't interested in having money in the bank, anyway, especially people like us who already have security. That's just it. We don't know what it's like to have our livelihood threatened, or to go hungry, or to have to wait for things we really need.'

Lance grunted. ' Our parents don't give us the chance to find out, and they think they're doing us a favour by it.'

' Well, they are! And all the great charters have words like " freedom from want " in them.'

' I *know*—and of course, one wouldn't voluntarily go hungry, but on the whole, I think I value independence, the freedom to make my own mistakes, more than I value having everything handed to me on a plate,' Lance protested vehemently.

' Very fine sentiments, I'm sure, young man,' came a voice from the doorway.

Lance and Kate swung round to see Eric Martham standing there. He didn't look very pleased, and the sarcasm in his voice had not gone unnoticed by Kate.

' There's something you should remember, Lance,' he went on. ' It's one thing admiring the snow with your back to a roaring fire, it's quite another having to fight your way through it day after day. In other words, it's all very well talking about independence and freedom to make your own mistakes from the security of a good home, it's quite another starting from scratch in a competitive world. You don't know how lucky you are. Why don't you let your father help you and be thankful? It's natural for a father to want to save his son from making the same mistakes and having quite such a struggle. You'll have plenty of opportunities for making your own decisions—*and* mistakes—as the years go by.'

Lance had risen from his seat. ' Yes, I—suppose you're right, Mr Martham.'

' Of course I am, my boy, and don't you forget it,' Eric Martham said gruffly. He put his hand in his pocket and held out a five pound note. ' Here, if you two are going out for the day, have lunch or something on me. Go on, take it, and don't be so silly,' he urged as Lance hesitated. ' After all, you're doing me a favour taking Kate out of the way.'

He grinned and Kate laughed with him. ' Come on, Lance, let's go—and if you don't take the fiver, I will.'

' Now you're talking sense,' her father said, and thrust the note into Lance's hand. ' Enjoy yourselves,' he added as he went out of the door.

Lance sighed and looked ruefully at the note. ' He shouldn't have, you know.'

' Well, he wanted to, obviously. At a guess, I'd say he realized he had no right to lecture you like that, really, and that was his way of apologizing. Anyway, you took it very well—the lecture, I mean. You deserve some compensation.'

' His motives were good, at least,' Lance said as they went out to his car. ' The trouble is, the parents are so nearly always right. I suppose if I valued my freedom and independence all that much, I'd cut loose from home altogether. But then they would be hurt, especially Mother.'

Kate settled in the car beside him. Both she and Lance had their own cars. Would they if they didn't work for their parents?

' It's your decision, Lance,' she said quietly. ' I imagine one's parents always feel it when their offspring leave home, whether it's to get a job, see the world, have a place of their own or get married. Suppose your father *did* buy an existing small boathire business and

63

wanted to put you in it, would you take it?'

' I don't know. What do you think?'

' I think it would be a jolly good idea. If you wanted to, you could gradually buy it from him. I feel sure he'd agree to that. Wouldn't he?'

Lance nodded. ' I think so. But I'm not at all sure that I want to settle down in the boathire business.'

' Lance!' Kate exclaimed in a shocked voice. ' Why ever not?'

He did not answer for a moment; when he did he said quietly, ' That I can't tell you, Kate. Let's talk about something else—if we can. Tell me about that Thornton fellow. Have you seen him again since Saturday?'

She gave him a sidelong glance. ' That isn't much of a change of subject, Lance, when it was partly his fault that your father was refused planning permission.'

' I wasn't thinking of him in that connection. I was thinking of him as a new personality in the area. I rather suspect Millie is seeing him. She seems very elusive these days.'

Something inside Kate contracted sharply. ' Millie? Seeing Lee Thornton? What on earth gave you that idea?'

' Why the astonishment? It's not so improbable. She soon got into conversation with him that night at the Wherry. When Millie sets her mind to anything nothing will stop her.'

' Possibly. But I'm sure you're just jumping to conclusions.'

' Not without reason,' he answered doggedly.

' Have you—seen them together?' asked Kate.

' No.'

' Then—' Kate paused and frowned—' what made you say she was elusive? Have you been trying to contact her?'

' Well, yes, once or twice.' He flicked Kate a glance.

'Did you say whether you'd seen anything of Thornton or not?'

'A couple of times by accident,' she told him.

'Find out anything more about him?' he enquired casually.

Kate laughed shortly. 'Our brief meetings have ended in crossed swords.'

'What about?'

She affected a shrug. 'Oh, the usual controversy. The Broads. But I met his mother the other day. She came to the shop. She's a charming woman.'

Lance made no comment, but fell silent as he drove towards Norwich. Kate lapsed into silence too, thinking further of Lee's mother, then of Lee himself, her heart becoming heavy as she wondered if what Lance suspected was true—that Lee and Millie were going out together. Millie was a very attractive girl. She had that beautiful translucent skin which often accompanied Titian hair. She was bright and lively, and most important of all, she had no great opinions about subjects like the future of the Broads. If she had, she would be clever enough not to voice them too strongly if they clashed with those of someone with whom she wanted to be on good terms.

Kate sighed. If only she had been more like Millie! But then her father was so against Lee, too. And even if he wasn't, her thoughts went on, the situation might not be any different. Lee appeared not to like her. Another sigh escaped her.

Lance glanced at her. 'What's the matter?'

Kate grimaced. 'Oh, you know—all this Broads business. I don't blame you for wanting to get away.'

'Would you come with me?' he asked swiftly.

She laughed shortly. 'Don't tempt me.'

'Are you really tempted?' he asked quietly.

She thought for a moment, then answered: 'It's always a temptation to run away from a difficult situation, Lance, isn't it? If you're asking me seriously, how could I possibly go away and leave Father on his own?'

'You've certainly got a problem there,' he said thoughtfully. 'But there might come a time when you'll have to come to a decision, and I'm sure your father would never stand in the way of your happiness.'

'Oh, he wouldn't,' she agreed swiftly.

She was not quite sure where the conversation was leading, however, or what Lance had in mind, so she thought it better to bring it to an end.

'Where are we going?' she asked as they passed a part of the old ruined wall of the city. 'Are we having lunch in Norwich?'

'I think we might as well, don't you? Then I thought we'd take a run out to Thetford Chase. It will be nice to see lots of trees instead of lots of water for a change.'

'A good idea. I love the forest.'

She loved Norwich, too, always had. It was a beautiful old city, ancient and modern buildings living together with complete harmony, dominated by the Norman Castle and blessed by the Cathedral whose graceful spire soared high into the sky.

Lance left his car in one of the shoppers' car parks, and they had lunch in a restaurant which looked out on to the colourful market. To the left was the beautiful Parish Church of Norwich, St Peter Mancroft: on the right the fifteenth-century Guildhall built in grey stone and flint, and overlooking the market from a slight rise was the modern City Hall, a very fine building indeed, its clock tower rising to one side some two hundred feet. The covers of the market stalls were in every conceivable colour—blue, yellow, pink, green, red and white stripes, orange. It was as gay and colourful a scene as anything which could be seen on the Continent.

They had rather a special lunch on Eric Martham's generosity, but even so there was a pound or so change.

66

Lance insisted on Kate having that.

'Put it towards a new dress or something,' he suggested. 'I don't want your father to pay for the whole of the day's outing. After all, I asked you out.'

Kate smiled absentmindedly. A new dress might not be such a bad idea. She wore slacks and sweaters far too often.

'Did you say something about dancing later on?' she asked.

He nodded. 'Either that or a film, but I don't think there's anything very special on just now that we haven't already seen. So we'll go dancing if you feel like it.'

'Yes, I think I do feel like it—and I'll buy that dress. I can put this money you're forcing on to me in my account. If I get a dress now, it'll save me going back home to change.'

She spent more on the dress than she intended, a sweet, intensely feminine dress in misty blue with a frill which circled the low V-neck and continued in a tracery all the way down to the hem. Lance was very enthusiastic about it indeed, but Kate was thinking of Lee as she gazed at herself in the full-length mirror.

She had the dress packed in a box, and after booking a table for the evening, Lance drove the thirty or so miles to the acres of forestry called Thetford Chase. It was very peaceful and the oaks and chestnuts which flanked the pines were a soft spring green. They left the car at one of the special picnic areas and walked beneath the trees. Lance took her hand, and later, when they sat down to rest he covered her lips with his. Kate did not mind Lance kissing her, but she felt no emotion of the kind she should have done had she been in love.

'What's the matter, Kate?' he said after a minute or two. 'You're as stiff as a poker.'

'Sorry, Lance, I—can't help it.'

He sighed and got to his feet. 'Let's go, then. Are

you sure you feel like dancing tonight?'

'Of course I'm sure. But if you don't want to—'

He didn't answer. He took her hand again and they walked back to the car.

'Tea in Thetford, then back to Norwich?' he queried as he started the engine.

'Fine.'

She wondered how much longer this special friendship they had so far enjoyed could survive if Lance continued to want more affection from her than she could give him. But loving Lee as she did, only ordinary friendship was going to be possible now, with either Lance or any other man.

Later, when she changed her dress at the place where they were dining and dancing, she could not help wishing that Lee could see her in the dress. It suited her so perfectly.

But it was Lance whose compliments she had to accept when she joined him, and from the special way he looked at her throughout the meal, she began to wonder whether she had been wise to wear it.

They had reached the last course when she saw his eyes widen as he glanced across the room.

'Good heavens!'

'What's the matter?' she asked.

'Over there, third table from the band.'

Kate looked and her heart lurched. It was Lee, and with him was Millie.

CHAPTER IV

'Can you beat that?' Lance muttered darkly.

Kate forced her gaze slowly away and, suppressing her feelings with a great effort, said casually:

'Well, they have a perfect right to be here, Lance.'

Lance gave her a fierce look. 'That's a pretty inane remark, Kate, if I may say so. You know perfectly well what I'm driving at. He hasn't been in the area more than five minutes, as you might say, and he's much too old for her. I don't like it at all, and I wouldn't have thought you would, either. Millie's your friend as much as she's mine.'

Kate eyed him with puzzled amusement. 'Really, Lance, anyone would think he was old enough to be her father and was abducting her or something!'

'Well, he does have a bad reputation. The woman I saw him with that evening looked much older and more sophisticated than Millie. He's a fast worker—and I don't like it. Do you?' he demanded.

Kate took a deep breath. 'No, I can't say I do,' she said with heartfelt honesty. 'But I don't see how you can lay all the blame at his door—if blame is the right word. Millie liked him right from the start.'

'She made believe she did, anyway.'

If Lance had not wanted to marry herself, Kate would have suspected him of being jealous of Lee.

'Do you—think we should ask them to join us?' she asked tentatively. 'It would seem the natural thing as we're such friends of Millie's. They might not want to, of course.'

She baulked at saying *they might want to be alone*. She waited for Lance's answer, not sure herself whether she wanted to join the other two.

'It wouldn't be a bad idea at that,' Lance muttered. 'Not that I want *his* company. Anyway, let's dance, shall we? Maybe they haven't seen us yet.'

It was a popular, romantic tune. The lights were lowered and already there were a number of couples on the dance floor. When Lance and she passed the table where Millie and Lee had been sitting it was empty, and later Kate had a glimpse of them dancing. But as they sat down again at the end of the dance a waitress came to their table with a note. It was from Lee asking if they would care to join Millie and himself for a drink.

'Shall we go?' Lance asked.

Kate nodded, and her heart beating in a peculiar rhythm, she walked with him across the room.

Lee rose as they approached. 'Well, well, it's a small world, so they say.'

'Not really,' Lance answered. 'This *is* the best place in Norwich for dancing with a meal.'

Lee's eyebrows raised a little. 'Do sit down, Kate, and tell me what you'd like to drink. You too—er— Lance, is it?'

Realizing that the two had never actually met, Kate made the introduction. Millie did not look very pleased, and it occurred to Kate that she probably would have preferred to have Lee to herself. But if that were the case why should Lee have asked them?

Their drinks were served and Millie asked Kate if today had been her day off as usual.

'Of course, " days off " don't worry me,' she added rather cattily—unusually so, for her. 'I can just go when and where I please.'

'So can I,' Kate said quietly. 'I *prefer* to help Father, and Wednesday happens to be one of our less busy days.'

Millie smiled and shrugged as if Kate were 'splitting hairs'. Kate noticed that she was looking particularly well dressed, but much quieter than usual in grey and white as if she were trying to look older—which she probably was for Lee's sake.

'Well, what have you been doing with yourself all day?' Lee asked Kate.

Kate began to tell him briefly, then the music started again and almost immediately he asked her to dance. She hesitated momentarily, then rose. A change of partners was inevitable, she supposed.

It was a strange experience, one hand enclosed in his, the other resting on his shoulder, and the slight pressure of his hand on her waist. Strange but wonderful. He moved well and she followed him easily, glad that she had learned some ballroom dancing. He did not speak for a while, and after searching vainly in her mind for something original to say, she gave up and just enjoyed the close proximity of him, their limbs moving together in blissful harmony.

'A new dress?' he asked unexpectedly as they stood and applauded when the music stopped.

'Why, yes. How did you guess?'

'Easily. I saw you and Lance going into the shop this afternoon.'

'Did you? I didn't see you.'

'I could tell that—and I had someone with me too. It suits you,' he added, as she was wondering whom he had had with him.

She gave a smile of pleasure. 'Thank you.'

'It matches your eyes,' he added with a suggestion of humour as if he did not want her to take him too seriously.

She laughed lightly. 'Such compliments!' then before she could stop herself: 'But perhaps you should save them for Millie.'

The music started again, without saying anything he led her into the encore.

Kate could have kicked herself. It was a perfectly ridiculous thing to come out with.

'Now, what made you say that, I wonder?' he queried after a moment or two.

Kate tried to save her face. 'It's—just that it seems rather odd for you to be paying compliments to someone else when you're—' She broke off, not being sure how to put it. But he wasn't to let her off.

'When I'm what?' he demanded.

'You know perfectly well what I mean.'

'I do not. They could hardly even be called compliments. I simply remarked that your dress suited you and that it matched your eyes—which is perfectly true. Your eyes *are* blue. A sort of misty, May morning blue,' he added, leaning back his head and looking into her eyes as if to confirm his statement.

She coloured and looked away. 'How ridiculous!'

She had the feeling that he was laughing at her, trying mildly to flirt with her and remembered with added discomfiture his 'reputation'.

'Why ridiculous?' he pursued.

'I would prefer you not to say things you don't mean,' she answered coolly.

'I'll remember that in future,' he told her, a hint of sarcasm in his voice.

He became silent, and perversely she wanted to continue the subject.

'Why did you use the phrase—misty May morning blue?' she asked.

His dark brows arched. 'Ah! So you liked the simile, really.'

'Well, it was—different. You *could* simply have called them pale blue.'

'I could.'

'Then—'

'You're very persistent, aren't you? I suppose the

72

phrase came into my mind because of the way you came at me through the mist the morning you—nearly knocked a hole through my boat.'

'Oh yes, of course.'

'Satisfied?'

She wasn't, quite, though what she would have liked him to say she wasn't sure. She sought her mind for a fresh topic of conversation, but the music came to an end and he led her back to his table. During the next dance which she had with Lance she could think of a dozen different things she would have liked to talk to Lee about.

'Do you want to stay with them or shall we go back to our own table?' Lance asked her.

It was a simple enough question, but Kate did not quite know how to answer it. There was a part of her which wanted so much to be with Lee, but there was also a part of her which shrank from the pain of knowing that if he did not actually dislike her, he preferred Millie. She was not normally jealous of her friends, but she loved Lee so much.

'I—I don't know,' she said in answer to Lance's question. Then her longing to be in Lee's company came uppermost. 'I think it would look rather rude if we left them now—and Millie might be hurt.'

Lance grunted sceptically. 'I wonder. Anyway, whether she would or not, I think a little competition wouldn't do him any harm.'

Kate couldn't quite understand Lance's attitude, but her mind was too occupied with Lee to give a great deal of thought to his motives. The party stayed together for the rest of the evening, and Kate found she was dancing with Lee more often than with Lance.

'You dance well,' he told her once. 'I thought ball-room dancing was a dying art with someone as young as you.'

73

Kate hated the emphasis on the difference in their ages, or even that he should infer it.

'Good heavens, I'm not as young as all that!' she retorted with a touch of annoyance.

'I'm sorry,' he said in the tone he might have used to placate a child.

'How old do you think I am, anyway?' she demanded.

He shrugged. 'I don't know. Eighteen?'

'I'm over twenty-one,' she told him. 'In fact, I'm twenty-two.'

'As old as that?' he murmured.

She felt he was laughing at her.

'And how old, may one ask, are you?'

'I'm over thirty.'

Her heart sank a little though she had guessed he was round about that age. She was determined, however, not to appear unduly impressed.

'As old as that?' she mocked.

He gave an amused smile. 'Tit for tat, eh? I must admit you're older than I thought, but you can hardly blame me for that.'

'What do you mean?'

'Simply that you look so much younger than you are.'

Kate did not know whether to take this as a compliment or not. On the whole she thought not.

But she said: 'Surely it isn't so much the way a person looks that matters?'

'True. And you do live a very simple, unsophisticated life, don't you?'

'And what's wrong with that?' she retorted.

'Nothing, nothing,' he assured her with a hastiness she did not altogether like. 'In fact, I find it very refreshing.'

Refreshing, simple, unsophisticated. All terms related to the very young, to which group she did not consider she belonged, and all of which still further emphasized

74

the gap in their ages.

'Is that what attracts you to Millie?' she shot out, to her immediate regret.

'Possibly,' he answered coolly.

When the evening was over Kate lost sight of Millie in the last-minute scramble for coats. When at last she went out into the foyer she found Lee waiting alone. There was no sign of Lance or Millie.

'Have you seen either of them?' Kate enquired of Lee.

'They've gone,' he told her.

'Gone? But that's not possible. They're probably waiting outside.'

'I can assure you they're not.'

Kate went to look herself, and Lee followed her. But there was still no sign of them.

'But this isn't like Lance. I can't understand it,' she said in a puzzled voice.

'He seems to have appointed himself Millie's—er—guardian. It was quite obvious that he didn't trust me to take her home.'

'But he didn't seem worried about me?'

'Perhaps he thinks you are less—susceptible to my bad influence,' he suggested with a smile of amusement.

Kate did not answer. She thought it very odd indeed that Lance should have brought her, but then left someone else to take her home without saying anything to her.

'He wanted to take you both home, actually,' said Lee, supplying part of the answer to her thoughts. 'But I talked him out of it. I was sure you wouldn't mind.'

'Oh, were you?' she answered indignantly.

He took her arm. 'Well, whether you do or you don't, there's no point in standing here. My car is in the car park.'

He marshalled her along to the side of the building where the car park was situated, and as the very last bus had probably gone a long time ago, Kate had no option but to go with him. But she still did not feel she had the whole story. No doubt she would get it from Lance.

As Lee drove in the direction of home Kate began to feel a little uneasy. What would her father say about Lee taking her home? He would certainly not be very pleased, and her explanation of how it came about would sound very weak indeed. How could Lance have done such a thing?

'I take it that you, Lance and Millie are all very good friends?' Lee enquired as he drove along.

'Oh yes. We've known each other for years. We've —sort of grown up together.'

'You don't really mind Lance taking Millie home?'

'I'm not jealous, if that's what you're driving at.'

'Oughtn't you to be?'

'What do you mean?'

But he answered her question with another. 'Aren't you engaged—or at any rate what's known as "going steady"?'

'We're not engaged. At least—'

'Yes?' he prompted.

But Kate did not feel she could go into details. 'Just that, actually. We're not engaged.'

'Does that mean you're free to accept other invitations out?' he queried.

'I suppose so. Why do you ask?'

'I might take a chance myself.'

Her heart gave a sudden turn about then righted itself as she remembered Millie and his reputation.

'Why might you?' she asked stiffly.

'Why not?'

'What about Millie?'

'I'm under no obligation to Millie.'

'No, but—'

76

'But what? Would you accept, if I did ask you?'

It was then she thought of her father again. 'I—don't know. I don't have to ask my father's permission, of course, but in view of your difference of opinion—'

'I see. It would be difficult for you. But otherwise, you wouldn't say no?'

'Er—no.'

'You don't sound very sure.'

'I'm not. It may interest you to know that your— reputation as a—a flirt arrived here well before you did.'

'Really?' he laughed. 'I can assure you there isn't an atom of truth in it.'

But Kate wasn't convinced. Not that she really minded about his reputation in one sense, but she could not bear the thought that she, too, would come under the heading of one of his affairs. She wanted to mean much more to him than that.

But he said no more on the subject, and she came to the conclusion he had merely been trying her out—perhaps for amusement.

'Will you tell your father I brought you home tonight?' he asked.

She frowned. 'Not—if I can help it,' she answered slowly.

'My name's still a red rag, I suppose?'

'Can you blame him?'

'I suppose not, though I haven't done him any actual harm.'

'Please, let's not go into that,' she asked of him. 'I only hope Father doesn't ask me anything about this evening, that's all.'

'But if he did you'd tell him the truth?' he probed.

'Of course. I'm not afraid of my father, I simply want to spare him any upset.'

'Does your father very easily get upset about things?'

'No. At least, he used not to, but he does seem extra

touchy these days, I don't know why. The business is doing well enough.'

Kate was sure there were several replies Lee could make to that, but was glad that he didn't.

As he neared the house, he asked: ' Would you like me to drive up as quietly as possible? Or even set you down a few yards off?'

She shook her head. ' Just normally, thanks. Lance doesn't always come in with me when we've been out, so Father might not make any comment.'

Lee stopped almost outside the front door. Kate turned to thank him for bringing her home, but before she could speak, he was out of the car to open the door for her.

' Goodnight, then, Kate,' he said, putting a hand on her shoulder.

' Goodnight, Lee—and thanks.'

He smiled and slammed the door on the passenger side. ' Sleep tight,' he added, pinching her cheek as if she were a schoolgirl.

He went and got into the driving seat, and Kate made her way to a side door they often used. Her father was in the living-room watching a documentary programme on television which was just finishing. He made one or two comments on it, then switched off.

' You came in very quietly. Had a nice day?'

She kissed him. ' Yes, thank you, Father, very nice. I bought a new dress. Like it?'

She took off her coat and swung around for him to see.

' Very nice indeed! I imagine Lance thinks so too, doesn't he?'

She nodded and gave him a brief account of the day, then asked him if he would like a drink and something to eat.

Lance, Lance, Lance, her thoughts went, and she

made her way into the kitchen. That was all her father seemed to want for her these days—to marry Lance.

She was taking her own drink to bed with her and was half way up the stairs when the telephone rang.

Her father was picking up the receiver before she could get to it, muttering: 'Who on earth can be ringing at this hour?'

Kate stood still on the stairs. Lance, she thought. It would be Lance, probably to apologize or explain. She prayed that he wouldn't ask her father if she had arrived home. She heard him say, 'Yes, she's here. I'll get her for you. Hang on a minute.'

He came to the bottom of the stairs and looked up at her with a broad smile.

'It's Lance. Don't you youngsters ever finish saying goodnight?'

Her fears subsided. She laughed and came down the stairs again. Her father disappeared into the living-room and discreetly closed the door behind him.

Kate picked up the receiver. 'Hello, Lance.'

'Oh, Kate, I hope it was all right leaving Thornton to take you home.'

'It's all right—so far,' she answered guardedly. 'But it was a very odd thing to do, wasn't it?'

'It was Thornton. He hustled us off, saying he was taking you home as if you'd already agreed and it was all arranged.'

'But he said you wanted to take Millie home.'

'The *two* of you—yes. You didn't mind, did you, Kate?'

'No, of course not, except that—' She glanced at the living-room door. 'I'll give you a ring some time tomorrow, Lance. Goodnight.'

She called out to her father and mounted the stairs again, her mind in an uneasy turmoil. Why had Lee wanted to take her home? Why had he wanted to know what her answer would be if he asked her out? Was it a game he played? If only he had shown signs of even remotely liking her, it wouldn't be so bad. But he hadn't. Not really. Even tonight they had argued a good deal of the time. At best his attitude was one of amused tolerance. And now that he had discovered she was not quite as young as he had imagined, he thought it safe to flirt mildly with her, to take her out. He was the kind of mature, attractive man who found young women of her age and Millie's, refreshing. Kate thumped her pillow angrily, but her heart ached unbearably as she settled down to sleep.

After lunch the following day, Eric Martham took out a motor launch saying he was going for a run to Ludham. Kate helped him to push off then wandered into the house with the vague idea of making a cake for the weekend. Friday tended to be a busy day. On Saturdays, of course, there was barely time to breathe, and her father loved homemade cakes. She quite forgot that she had promised to ring Lance until she heard a car pull up and Lance himself appeared in the doorway of the kitchen.

'Thought I'd just drop in,' he said cheerfully.

'Glad you did,' she answered, wondering at his change of mood since yesterday evening. 'I wanted to remind you not to say anything in front of Father about last night—Lee Thornton being at the Norwood Rooms and bringing me home afterwards. He'd be furious. Upset, anyway. I told you how Father had ordered him off, didn't I?'

'Lord, yes. Hope I didn't make things difficult for you, but I really think it worked as far as Millie's concerned.'

'How do you mean?'

'Well, I don't think she's all that keen on Thornton, after all.'

80

'What makes you say that?'

'Oh, just little things she said. I think he did most of the chasing, and of course she was hopping mad at the way he pushed her on to me.'

'If she isn't "all that keen" why was she mad? Maybe she was jealous. I think everybody's behaving very oddly these days, yourself included.'

Lance pulled a face. 'It's this Thornton bloke. He seems to have upset everybody's apple cart. You and your father, my father, myself of course, as well as Millie.'

'Hardly Millie. At least, not at first. Anyway, I've hardly seen her to ask how she does feel, and there wasn't much opportunity for private conversation last night.'

Lance looked at her curiously. 'How did you make out with Thornton? Whenever I glanced your way you were talking nineteen to the dozen. I shouldn't think he'd get his own way where you're concerned.'

Kate made no comment.

Then Lance said: 'By the way, Father's talking about buying a small boathire business. I rather thought he might.'

'Is there one on the market?'

'I don't know about "on the market" exactly. At least, I don't think there's one advertised, but of course Father has a way of knowing about these things almost before they're thought of.'

'Has he asked you if you're willing to manage a business of your own?' asked Kate.

Lance fiddled with a piece of string. 'He has, as a matter of fact, and I—said I would. I might as well. I don't really want to leave Norfolk—yet. It's just that I'm unsettled and a bit fed up at the moment. If I did decide to quit later I'm sure he could get a manager.'

Kate frowned. 'But he's doing it for you, Lance. If

you've told him you'll do it, I think you should be prepared to stick to it.'

'What—for good?'

'Well, for at least five years.'

Lance sighed. 'One of these days, I'll do what *I*
want.'

'Ah, but at present you don't know what that is, do
you?'

'It's not always easy, Kate.'

'I know. I once heard someone say that if you try
to please everybody, you end up by pleasing nobody,
least of all yourself. Best thing is to do what you feel is
right. That's sometimes different from what you want.'

'Such words of wisdom from one so young and beautiful,' he said lightly, giving her a hug.

He left shortly afterwards. Kate put her cake in the
oven and set the automatic timer, then went outside
again. She was helping a day boat to moor when Mrs
Thornton came alongside. Kate found mooring space
for her and gave her a hand in stepping ashore.

'How nice to see you again, Mrs Thornton.'

'And you, Kate. I was wondering—would you come
along to the house and have tea with me one day? I
know how busy you are, but perhaps Sunday—?'

Kate gave an involuntary smile of pleasure. 'Why,
that would be lovely. Thank you.'

'Good. I'm just popping into the shop. I'll see you
when I've done my shopping, if you're not too busy.'

'I won't be. Come to the house and have a cup of
tea with me. I usually have one about this time.'

It was only when she was putting on the kettle that
Kate became aware of her misgivings. What would her
father say about her going to the Thorntons' house? It
was all so silly, of course, and she was not in the habit
of keeping her whereabouts from him. They always told
each other where they were going, or where they had

been. She really would have to be firm about this, she told herself. Mrs Thornton had nothing to do with her son's views, and Kate was determined that nothing should spoil her friendship with the older woman.

All the same, she couldn't help being pleased when Mrs Thornton said she could only stay a short time, just long enough for a quick cup of tea. While all the controversy was still raging about the Broads Report she would rather not have to introduce her father to anyone connected with Lee.

'I saw your father yesterday,' Jane Thornton said. 'He came into the store while I was there and I asked the man serving me who he was. He looked younger than I had imagined.'

'Oh, I'm sure you would like him,' Kate said quickly.

'I'm sure I would. He looked a very nice sort of man. But "softly, softly", as the saying goes. Your father, I presume, still feels angry with Lee?'

'I—I think so. As well as Lee's article in the paper, there was the business of Lance's father being refused planning permission to develop some land below Yarmouth.'

'That would be—Mr Faulkner? And his son Lance is a close friend of yours?'

'Yes,' Kate said with a sigh.

'Lee was only doing his job, Kate,' Jane Thornton pointed out mildly.

'I know. At least, I suppose he was.'

'I don't think Lee knew the connection at the time,' Jane said thoughtfully. 'All the same, he's not the man to let himself be influenced unduly. He says and does what he feels to be right. I'm not saying he *is* always right, of course,' she added swiftly, 'but he does feel very strongly about this business of nature conservation.'

'And Father feels equally strongly that a beauty spot like the Broads should be enjoyed by as many people as possible,' Kate rejoined defensively. 'But he isn't as commercially minded as Lee seems to think. *He* wouldn't like to see the Broads spoilt by over-development, either.'

'My dear, I'm sure he wouldn't,' placated Jane Thornton. 'And I don't think for a moment that Lee *does* consider your father commercially minded, but there are prejudices to be broken down on both sides, don't you agree?'

Kate nodded rather miserably, then a wry smile curved her lips. 'Father almost accused Lee of being a "long-haired idealist" the other day.'

Jane Thornton laughed, 'Oh dear!'

'You'll be pleased to hear I defended him. I said that at least he didn't have long hair.'

The older woman rose. 'I'm sure we shall succeed in bringing the two of them together one of these days—and in the process, bring about a better understanding of the differing viewpoints in the area about the future of the Broads. I should think it's essential that the idealist and the business men find a common bond—if that doesn't sound too impossible.'

Kate walked with her to the staithe. 'At the moment I feel like a buffer between the two.'

They stood for a moment at the waterside chatting and enjoying the long view across the Broad, the trees in their fresh spring green mirrored in the clear water.

'Sunday is all right for you, then, is it?' Jane asked as she prepared to leave. 'About four?'

Kate nodded. She would have to face any disapproval from her father.

'Yes, I'll be there—and thanks.'

As she spoke she saw her father's boat skimming across the Broad toward them.

'Here's Father,' she said swiftly, as Jane stepped into her launch.

'Well, I'll be off,' Jane answered. 'Give me a push out, will you, Kate? I'll start up the engine when I'm clear.'

Fortunately the engine started at first pull and Jane was away before Eric Martham reached the part of the staithe reserved for their private use. Kate strolled over to take his mooring rope, not necessary, but a courtesy.

He thanked her, then gazed across the Broad shading his eyes from the sun.

'Who was that woman you were talking to just now?' he asked.

CHAPTER V

Kate took a deep breath. She had never told deliberate lies to her father and she was not going to start now. Even evasions would probably lead to further questions so that in the end she would still have to tell him the truth.

'She's—Mrs Thornton, Father,' she said, half hoping the name would not fully register, or that he would not connect her with the man he had ordered off his premises.

But he frowned and turned his head slowly and looked at her.

'Thornton?' he repeated. 'She isn't any relation to that fellow—'

'Yes, Father, she is. As a matter of fact she's his mother.'

'His mother! You must be joking. For one thing, she doesn't look old enough.'

'And for another?' prompted Kate, eyeing him quizzically, hardly able to believe that she had not received an angry outburst from him.

'For another, she looks altogether too charming to be that fellow's mother.'

Kate suppressed a smile. 'You saw quite a lot from a distance.'

'I've seen her before, actually—in the shop. When did you find out who she was?'

'Oh, one day when she came shopping. She seems to buy most of her grocery and greengrocery from us.'

'You didn't say anything to me about her.'

'I was afraid you'd be angry—and she's such a nice woman.'

'Too nice from the look of her to be the mother of—' He broke off. 'I'm repeating myself. I just think it's a pity that she's *his* mother, that's all.'

He turned and went into the office. Kate looked after him with some amusement. Perhaps it wouldn't be so difficult to reconcile Lee and her father, after all. But a moment later a sense of acute depression came over her. Even if they were, what possible difference would it make to the way Lee regarded herself? In any case, on second thoughts both her father and Lee were far too strong in their views ever to change them very easily.

Somewhat reluctantly Kate went along to the Wherry on Saturday evening after the last of the holiday-makers had taken over their craft or houseboats. Until recently she had looked forward to these evenings with her friends. Now she was half afraid Lee might be there with Millie or perhaps with the other woman with whom Lance had seen him. Even Lance's company was punctuated these days with awkward or uneasy conversation. But most important of all, perhaps, she felt she herself was changing. Evenings spent in the company of friends her own age, lively, sometimes boisterous, suddenly did not have the same appeal, partly because her inclinations were to moon around, thinking of Lee.

There was the usual kind of crowd in the brightly lit room. Yachtsmen, cruiser skippers, anglers, girls in a variety of slacks, trouser suits and gay sweaters, and here and there a few locals eyeing the visitors, for the most part with either tolerant or slightly scornful amusement. But Millie was not there at all, which was even worse than seeing her with Lee.

'What's happened to her, I wonder?' she queried, though afterwards she wished she hadn't. To Lance it was a foregone conclusion.

'What do you think?' he countered. 'She's with Thornton, I expect.'

'Not necessarily.'

'I don't know what you're so worried about,' Tony

Sheldrake said to him. ' I admit he's no great friend of us boathire people, but Millie's father is a *boatbuilder*— and he's selling more overseas than he is for Broads use, so Thornton's views don't affect him. Anyway, he looks a decent enough bloke. Why shouldn't she go out with him? None of us here have any prior claim on her.'

' I know that,' answered Lance. ' But as I've said before, we *are* her friends, and I think she's heading for trouble.'

' What kind of trouble?' queried Lindy mischievously.

' I mean that she stands a good chance of getting hurt,' he said with slow emphasis.

' That's her own look-out, isn't it?' put in David Lines mildly.

' Well, that's a nice thing to say, I'm sure!' Lance protested indignantly.

' Hold your horses,' said Tony, who was sitting facing the door. ' Here comes Millie now—and she's on her own.'

Another chair was brought up and a space made for her.

' And where's the great Romeo?' queried Tony, receiving a glare from Lance.

' I presume you're referring to Mr Thornton?' Millie said haughtily. ' Well, if you must know, he's away for the week-end.'

The talk and the teasing went on. Kate was thinking that if Lee were away she would not see him when she went to tea, and she wondered if that was why his mother had asked her on that particular day.

Presently Lindy, David and Tony, left to go to a local dance. Neither Kate nor Millie wanted to go, and although Kate said she would be going home soon as she had had a particularly hard day, Lance insisted on staying with Millie and herself.

After the others had gone, Millie said she was hungry. 'Lance, be an angel and rustle up a sandwich or something,' she pleaded.

He rose at once. 'Anything for you, Kate?'

But Kate shook her head. When he had gone to the bar, Millie asked:

'How'd you make out with Lee the other night?'

Kate winced. Millie's phraseology was a little crude at times.

'What do you mean? He drove me home and that was that.'

'Didn't he ask you out?'

'No, he didn't,' Kate answered, truthfully as it happened.

'Oh. Oh, well, that's something,' Millie said with obvious relief. 'You didn't mind, did you?'

'Mind what? That he didn't ask me out?'

'No, I mean—mind *his* taking you home instead of Lance.'

'I wasn't annoyed, if that's what you mean, but I thought it a bit odd.'

Millie shrugged. 'Lee said he wanted to talk to you and gave the impression that it was important. I thought perhaps it had something to do with this Broads Report business. Either that or he wanted to see you again. He does have a certain reputation, as I told you when he first came.'

'In that case, I'm surprised you're having anything to do with him,' Kate said woodenly.

Millie shrugged. 'Are you? I think he's exciting. To tell you the truth I'm finding some of these *boys* around here rather tedious.'

'They're not boys, they're men,' Kate told her with a hint of annoyance.

'Well, you wouldn't think so the way they go on. Look at Lance—at the beck and call of his father.

89

Father says jump and Lance jumps. He doesn't seem to have a mind of his own at all.'

'That's not fair!' Kate protested warmly. 'And you know it.'

'I don't know it,' retorted Millie. 'And I don't think you do either. You're only springing to his defence because you think you ought to.'

Fortunately, perhaps, Lance returned with a plate of sandwiches.

'I think I can peck a bit,' he said when Millie remarked on the stack. 'And I'm sure Kate will find room for one or two.'

But Kate rose to her feet. 'I promised Father I wouldn't be late. Hope you don't mind, Lance. Don't bother to get up or see me home. My car's outside.'

She said a hurried goodnight and left them, wishing she had not come and thinking it was time to break the 'Saturday night at the Wherry' habit. For a few minutes she felt almost as Lance had done—like getting right away and finding fresh surroundings and a new beginning. Since meeting Lee her mind seemed to have been in a constant state of turmoil.

Her father was not in when she arrived home. There was a note on the kitchen table saying he had gone round to see Jim Faulkner and might be late. Kate sighed and all at once felt a loneliness she had never known before. Were she and her father gradually drifting apart or were they each beginning to feel the lack of a partner, a second self, that special relationship which could only exist between a man and a woman, a husband and wife?

She tried to dismiss such thoughts. What was the use of dwelling on them? Her father was still too much in love with the memory of her mother to think seriously of another woman. As for herself, Lance could never be her 'second half', only Lee. And Lee did not even remotely care for her.

The next morning Eric Martham slept late. Kate was not sure whether to tell him she was having tea with Mrs Thornton or not. She was cooking Sunday lunch when he came downstairs moody and withdrawn, somehow, as if he had something on his mind. He wandered outside and took a rowing boat out on to the Broad. At lunch he was silent for the most part, answering Kate only briefly, then outside he went again. Kate did the washing up then followed him, wondering how to tell him where she was going and how he would react. He might think going to the Thornton's was tantamount to disloyalty on her part.

There were one or two cars parked near the café/milk bar, not an unusual sight when the weather was fine, and in midsummer the parking lot was often crammed full. A number of the day boats were out on hire too, and Kate was beginning to wonder if she really could be spared.

'Do you think we're going to be very busy, Father?' she asked.

He looked at her rather vaguely. 'Why? Do you want to go off somewhere?'

'Well, yes, but—'

'Then off you go. I shall manage.'

He moved away as a six-berth cruiser looked to be having difficulty in bringing the craft in to moor. Kate went indoors to change. Would he even notice if she did not wear her customary slacks and sweater? She found a plain white skirt which she had not worn for a long time. It was rather shorter than today's fashion, but when she put it on to see how it looked, she liked it. Perhaps she ought to wear her clothes a little shorter now. Topped by a light pink sweater the outfit looked quite smart. She felt sure Lee's mother would approve.

Outside, she called out to her father that she was going, and he came to give her a push off, but he did not ask where she was going. Kate rowed clear of the other craft then thought she might as well hoist sail. Turning the boat nose to wind, she tied the rudder amidships while she unfastened the sail ties, then topped the boom, and with an ease and skill born of a great deal of practice, hoisted the sail without a hitch. The sight of the unfurled canvas tempted her to take one or two runs across the Broad and back, and she couldn't help wondering whether Lee could sail or whether he always used a motor launch. 'If you haven't sailed a boat, you haven't lived,' she often said to people who preferred power to sail.

But it was nearly four now, so she steered towards the entrance of the Broad. Up the creek progress was a little slow, for although the wind was in the right direction it was only quite a light one and much of it was blanketed off by trees. One advantage of sailing over rowing was that in sailing you faced the way you were going, and as she made her way slowly along she saw Mrs Thornton come out of the house and walk down to the water's edge. Kate waved, and in a few minutes she had turned into wind and brought the *Aerial* gently to moor.

'Well done!' Jane Thornton called out.

Kate jumped ashore and made fast. 'Sorry I was so slow. It didn't seem worth while lowering sail—and I doubt if I'd have been much quicker on the oars.'

'Don't apologize. It was lovely to watch you. I rather wish I could sail.'

'I could easily teach you.'

Jane smiled. 'Thank you, Kate. I might take you up on that one day. Come in and see the house.'

The motor launch used by both Lee and his mother was moored at the staithe, so Kate thought it probable that Lee did not sail either. Mrs Thornton went on talking about the house, so Kate did not like to interrupt by asking her.

'We both hate the name,' she was saying. 'The Grange. Ugh! I think we shall call it Thornton House. What do you think?'

'Why not Thornton Hall?' suggested Kate.

'That sounds a little grand, don't you think?' Jane answered with a laugh.

But Kate didn't think so. 'I'm sure the house is big enough for the title. At least, it looks it from the out-side.'

'It *is* rather on the large side,' Jane admitted. 'But that's one reason why we got it so cheaply. People don't like big houses nowadays. And of course, it was in a very bad state of disrepair, especially inside. What we've done is make one or two rooms fit to live in, and we'll do the rest gradually.'

She led the way to a large French window which opened directly into a large lounge-hall.

'This is really the nicest room in the house,' she told Kate, 'and fortunately was in the best state. The plaster work is particularly fine. The staircase is very attrac-tive, too.'

She pointed to the hand-carved newel post and curving banister, but it was the lounge-hall itself which interested Kate most. The ceiling with its beautifully modelled centre-piece, the leaf and fruit mouldings which divided the ceiling into rectangles and the deep cornice which had the same motif repeated on its principal members. Plain ordinary ceilings were all Kate had ever seen except in stately homes. The walls were beautifully panelled, ovals set into rectangles, but what struck her particularly were two rounded and curved alcoves which simply called out for marble or bronze statues to be housed in them.

'Yes, indeed,' Kate murmured. 'Beautiful.'

Jane smiled. 'I must say it all looked very depressing when Lee first brought me to see it. There were horrible dust marks on the walls where pictures had been hung, the woodwork was dull and grimy, and of course you couldn't see the cornice work for cobwebs. So we had this room done before we moved in—this and the kitchen. That needs remodelling. But I'm afraid we couldn't afford to have the whole place done. We shall have to do the rest ourselves by degrees.'

'Why did you buy such a big place—if there's only you and Lee?' queried Kate.

'We liked the location and Lee said it was the kind of house he'd always had a yen for.' She laughed. 'I'm afraid Lee isn't the country cottage type. He likes plenty of room. But he has plans for shutting off the top of the house altogether—at least, more or less. He'll just leave access for repairs. Then he'll insulate the floor as if it were the ceiling. Otherwise it will cost the earth to heat. But Lee's main idea is to convert part of the first floor into a self-contained flat for me so that when he gets married I shall still be able to live here. Whether it will materialize I don't know. It will depend on what his wife feels, but Lee says any woman who doesn't agree won't be the kind of woman he wants to marry.'

'He's—not engaged, then?' asked Kate.

Jane Thornton smiled and shook her head. 'Not yet. I have an idea the day is fast approaching, though.'

Kate swallowed hard. 'Do you—think he's met someone?'

'Yes, I think he has.'

'But suppose when Lee puts the situation to her—about your flat—and she doesn't like the idea? If he really loves her—'

Jane shrugged. 'My dear, don't ask me to sort it out. He's convinced that she'll be all for the idea.'

'Would you like it yourself?' asked Kate.

'I don't see why not. It's a big enough house, the

walls and the floors are thick and fairly soundproof. If necessary, additional soundproofing is easy enough. But it isn't settled yet, by any means. It's just an idea Lee has. What do you think of it yourself?'

'I think Lee is right. No decent girl or woman could possibly object to such an arrangement. And I couldn't see him falling in love with someone who wasn't—well, a nice person.' Then she smiled. 'Of course it might not work with everyone. Not all mothers-in-law would be like you—pleasant, charming, easy to get along with—'

Jane laughed. 'Such compliments! But I'm glad you think so, anyway. A lot does depend on the various individuals, naturally. There are some types of woman one wouldn't want to have in the same street, still less in the same house. But come and have a look upstairs.'

The house had ten bedrooms of various sizes, some, Kate supposed, having been used as dressing rooms.

'Well, as you can see,' Jane said, 'there's enough space here for a self-contained flat, a nursery suite or anything you like.'

'Yes, indeed. And the second floor?'

'Servants' quarters, I expect. And storage. Not to mention the cistern room.'

'I wonder somebody hasn't wanted to buy it to convert it into a country club.'

'Not quite big enough, my dear. And too many structural alterations would have been needed. But let's go down and have some tea, then I'll show you the rest of the house. It's all ready, except for brewing the tea. You go and sit on the terrace—that is, if you'd like to have it outside.'

'Lovely.'

Canvas chairs and a wrought iron table had been placed outside. Kate sat and gazed across the lawn which swept down to the water's edge, and for a few minutes let her imagination run riot. How wonderful to live here as Lee's wife. What plans they would make, how happy they could be. She wouldn't shut off the top floor. She would make use of it. The view up there must be magnificent. Oh, Lee—Lee— Swiftly, her idyllic dreams turned to despair, and she was glad when Mrs Thornton came out with the tea tray.

'It really is beautiful here,' she sighed a little while later, soothed and brought to something like normal by the peace and quiet, the refreshing tea and the easy conversation of her hostess. 'Such a change from the constant comings and goings of people. I don't wonder at both the Major and Lee wanting to put a barrier across the entrance to the creek.'

'Well, it does bar the big cruisers who regard every strip of land as a mooring place. They'd probably take one look at the house and assume it was a hotel or something.' Jane eyed her questioningly. 'Don't you ever wish your place was—private?'

Kate frowned thoughtfully. 'Well—no, not really. Perhaps because I've been brought up with it as it is— busy, attracting a lot of people. If every beauty spot were private, it wouldn't be very nice for other people— the general public—would it? It can be very peaceful on Cocksfoot Broad in the early mornings and in the evenings when all craft are moored and settled down. And of course, it looks beautiful at any time with all the trees at the other side and the church spire behind. Even a motor cruiser or so moored over there somehow adds to the beauty.'

Jane nodded. 'It's a matter of what you're accustomed to, I expect—and I do agree that the beauty of the countryside shouldn't just be enjoyed by a few. All the same, you like it here?'

There was no doubt whatever about that. After tea they went inside again, and Jane showed Kate the rest

96

of the ground floor. The old domestic quarters were so extremely generous as to be sufficient for Lee and his mother to live in while the rest of the house was being renovated. The scullery was as big as the average modern kitchen and quite adequately housed cooker, sink, table and a generous supply of cupboards. The kitchen was huge and did double duty as dining and living room while another room, possibly used by a housekeeper, made a study/sitting room.

'Lee uses this room—he does a lot of writing of various kinds, and the old morning room makes a small sitting room for me. We feel it's a great thing to have privacy when you want it,' Jane Thornton said.

Kate glanced lingeringly around Lee's room. It was orderly, yet homely. On the desk was a typewriter and some open books, presumably for reference. There was a large bookcase, crammed with books, a large map of East Anglia on the walls and two of the Broads area. Beside the ornate fireplace was a roomy armchair, and a pipe rack set the seal of masculinity.

Kate was just admiring the drawing room—of magnificent proportions with two large floor-to-ceiling windows and a great white marble fireplace, supported by two female sculptured figures on either side, when there came the faint sound of a car braking and a moment later Lee himself appeared in the doorway. Kate's whole being leapt joyfully.

'Lee!' his mother exclaimed, holding out her hand in welcome. 'You're earlier than I expected. Have you had tea?'

'No, but I can wait if you've already had yours.'

'Nonsense. I'll make some more and you can have it while we talk to you. Finish showing Kate round while I go and see to it.'

She went out. Lee gave Kate an unfathomable look, then said gravely: 'Well, what do you think of it?'

'The—the house, you mean? I—think it's terrific,' she answered jerkily, then wondered if the word sounded too young.

He smiled and she was sure her fears were justified. 'I take it you don't mean that in the sense of the dictionary definition—" causing great terror ".'

Kate felt herself colouring, and her only defence was in anger, but she took a deep breath and forced it down, remembering that she was in his house.

'Why shouldn't we give new—and nicer—meanings to words?' she answered with sudden inspiration. 'It's a very colourful word and it means I'm enthusiastic about it. I think it has—terrific possibilities.'

His smile broadened. 'All right, you win. I'm glad you like it. Some people think we're crazy buying a great house like this. You—wouldn't think it too big then, for two?'

'Well, I—imagine there won't always be just the two of you,' she felt compelled to answer.

'That's true. Do you have ideas about houses? What, for instance, would you do with this room?'

She gazed all around. 'How would I furnish it, do you mean?'

'*And* the decor.'

Kate gazed up at the beautiful ceiling moulded in a Grecian key design and the panelled walls. 'I'd restore it to its former decor as far as possible and furnish it in the same period.'

'Antiques, you mean?'

'Not necessarily. That word is bandied about too much these days, I think. No, just—well, not ultra-modern stuff. This room will take large, comfortable chairs, huge settees one can lounge on. A concert grand piano.'

'Nothing elegant?' he queried.

She flashed a look at him. 'Yes, of course. Sheraton

or Chippendale—Hepplewhite—their work would show up to advantage in a room like this.' Her gaze strayed once more to the female figures on either side of the fireplace. ' I like these. Most unusual.'

He gave a reflective smile. ' Do you know the story behind those kind of figures?'

She shook her head. ' Tell me.'

' Well, they're called Caryatids after the women of Carya who were enslaved because of their betrayal of the Greeks to the Persians.'

' Oh dear! It sounds awful.'

He shrugged. ' Not necessarily. Some slaves— especially if they were young and beautiful were often treated very well by their masters. Pampered, you might say.'

' I think I'd prefer my freedom,' she answered.

' No doubt. Come and have a look at the library and dining room.'

There was not a great deal one could say about these two rooms. Here again, ornate fireplaces were the focal point and there was a great deal of interesting plaster work on the ceilings.

' Would you keep the dining room *as* a dining room?' Lee quizzed her.

' Oh yes, I think so. It would be lovely for dinner parties—plenty of room to get all around the table.'

' You'd like entertaining?'

' Yes, I think so. It's rather nice to have one's friends to a meal now and then.'

' I note you said friends.'

' Of course.'

' Then I take it you're not the kind of person who'd fill the house with people you don't know. It is done, you know, especially with the—younger generation.'

She kept herself severely in check. ' I know what you mean, but I never have liked that kind of party. What

99

about you?'

'Me?' he echoed as if surprised that she should ask. Then he smiled. 'Like you, I prefer to entertain my friends, rather than mere acquaintances. Though, of course, the occasional stranger is another matter. Shall we go outside now? It's a pity to miss the sunshine. It might not last.'

'What will you do with the library?' she asked as they went out on to the terrace. 'Have you the books to fill it in the old style?'

He shook his head. 'I wouldn't try. I do need more bookshelves than I have at present, but I wouldn't stack them from floor to ceiling. I shall use it as my study eventually. The small room I'm using now will make an excellent sewing or laundry room, don't you think?'

'Why, yes, I think it would.'

'It's so handy, I understand, for a woman to be able to just leave her dressmaking and shut the door on it rather than have to tidy up each time.'

Kate wondered from which woman he had gleaned this piece of information, and felt an unbearable envy towards the as yet unknown woman he was going to marry.

'I see you sailed up,' Lee remarked as they waited for Mrs Thornton to join them.

She turned to him eagerly. 'Do you sail, Lee?'

He gave a slight start and stared at her for a moment. Then he looked away again and answered: 'Not very much. I haven't had the opportunity. But I'm buying an ex-Broads auxiliary yacht, so I am hoping to do more. With an auxiliary, you get the best of all worlds, so they tell me.'

'That's true to a large extent, but it depends, really, on what rig you have. A gaff rig, for instance, with a loose-footed jib, can be a brute to manage on your own —and you don't always have a crew.'

He gave her a sly look. 'You're very knowledgeable. I suppose it comes of being "in the trade". What rig would you recommend, then?'

'Bermuda, with a self-acting jib,' she told him promptly. 'The sail goes up in a jiffy—once you know how—and the jib works without a crew. I—er—take it you're not going in for dinghy racing?'

'You take it correctly. I think the twists and turns of these rivers give quite enough excitement without racing.'

At this point Jane Thornton came out with a fresh pot of tea, full of apologies for the delay. 'There was I, waiting for the kettle to boil,' she told them, 'and I hadn't even switched it on. Now, what have you two been talking about?' she asked as she spread out the cups and saucers.

'House decorating and sailing,' Lee told her. 'And you're a cup short,' he added, eyeing the tea things.

'I thought I'd leave you to talk to Kate for a bit,' she said smoothly. 'I don't really want any more tea myself, and I've suddenly remembered I promised to ring Molly Cooper about going over there.'

Kate poured the tea, hoping Lee and herself would be able to keep clear of controversial subjects like the future of the Broads or nature conservation. Sailing, she decided, appeared to be the safest.

'Perhaps you'd like to try your hand with my half-decker,' she offered.

'Thanks, I'd like that. There's no jib at all with a lug sail, is there? I've always understood that it's impossible to sail without a jib. Even dinghies have one.'

She explained, feeling a sneaking satisfaction that, in spite of his being so much older than herself, and the superior attitude he adopted at times, sailing was something she *did* know more about than he did.

'It's the rig of a lug sail,' she told him. 'Part of it juts out forward of the mast and acts as a jib. It's a very clever idea, really. It might not be as efficient as a loose-fitting jib proper when it comes to turning on the tack, but for handling by one person, it's pretty good.'

'Mm. You certainly know your onions when it comes to sailing, don't you?'

She glanced at him suspiciously. Compliments were rare from him, and she did not consider herself an expert by any means. She replied modestly that she only knew about Broads sailing.

'And of course, I've had plenty of opportunity to learn,' she added.

'You could have become a speed-boat fiend,' he pointed out.

She smiled. 'Ah, but sailing is so much more fun, especially in the early spring when the breezes blow strong across the Broad and there are not many boat-hirers about. Wind power can often be far greater than mechanical power. I've overhauled, and passed, many a cruiser on the open river.'

As if he too considered sailing a safe subject of conversation, he told her the story of his first experience on Hickling Broad in hoisting the sail of a Broads yacht, which are much bigger than the average sailing dinghy.

'In retrospect it's funny, of course,' he said when he had finished, 'but at the time—well, it was hectic to say the least. And the friend I was on holiday with was no help at all. He knew less about the business than I did.'

There was a silence then, an almost happy, companionable silence. Kate treasured every fleeting moment, knowing that any second it could come to an end, and not daring to wonder whether he shared her own feeling of contentment. Or, if he did, whether it was anything or nothing to do with her own presence, but due entirely to the peace and quiet of the surroundings, the effect of the still-warm afternoon sun.

It was Lee who broke the silence. ' Do you think your father would object to my trying out my yacht on Cocksfoot Broad when I get it?' he asked.

Kate winced at the unpleasant reminder of the estrangement existing between Lee and her father.

' Strictly speaking, the Broad has been declared a public waterway,' she told him. ' In any case, he probably wouldn't recognize you, and if he did, he'd hardly bellow out over the Broad.'

' I suppose not. I'm only sorry I angered him so much in the first place. Do you think he'll ever—change towards me?'

' You make him sound so difficult—and he isn't. I suppose it depends on—what happens in Broadland during the next few months or so.'

The air had suddenly become charged. In an effort to restore their former comradeship which was in danger of being shattered again, Kate asked him if he'd like to try out the *Aerial* right away.

' Actually, I think there's a little more breeze now,' she said, lifting up her chin to the feel of it. ' And it's shifted more to the west. You might even sail down the creek.'

He accepted swiftly, and carried the tea tray indoors before following Kate down to the water's edge. A kind of nervous excitement held her which she tried to hide by concentrating on the general manœuvres of getting away. She invited Lee to hoist the sail and herself untied the clove hitch from round the mooring post and held it with a loose loop for getting away. A strange boat is like a strange car, or piano or other article, but she noticed that Lee only required the few necessary words on handling an unfamiliar piece of equipment before he had the sail hoisted, and roughly at the right setting for gliding gently down the creek.

'You're right,' he told Kate. 'She handles well and very easily. Are there many boats of this kind around?'

'Not a lot. You have to hunt around.'

'Then I might do that.'

'Do you mean—to have instead of the auxiliary you're thinking of buying?'

'I don't know. Perhaps in addition to. I imagine you have a need for different kinds of boats when you actually live on the Broads or rivers. For me, as for most people, it would depend how much they cost.'

'You might pick up some bargains at the autumn sale—if you can wait that long.'

Harmless conversation, every word of it precious to Kate. But once or twice he was careless with his steering and nearly caught the sail in the topmost branches of some of the trees.

'You might have to have some of those lopped, if you're going to do much sailing,' she told him.

He hauled in the mainsheet, and in doing so, lost wind. 'This, of course, is where a jib sail would be beneficial,' he said.

'Always remembering that, alone, you only have two hands, one of which you need for steering, the other for controlling the mainsheet,' she answered more sharply than she intended.

'One wouldn't always be alone,' he pointed out.

Kate did not answer. They were in danger of arguing again.

Out of the creek Lee steered on to Cocksfoot Broad. Kate glanced at the distant staithe, but could not see her father and decided that, sitting low in the boat as Lee and herself were, it was very doubtful that he would recognize them from this distance.

Lee made one or two turns across the width of the Broad then did a few tacks against the wind. Watching him from her seat in the centre of the half-decker, Kate came to the conclusion that he knew more about sailing than he had indicated. He was turning, the sail flapping idly, when a launch headed towards them. At first Kate couldn't see properly because of the sail, but as Lee straightened the craft and the sail filled, Kate found herself looking straight into the angry face of her father from the launch. His eyes blazing, he looked from one to the other, then turned and made back to the staithe without a word.

CHAPTER VI

'I'm sorry,' Lee said.

'That's all right. It's not your fault,' Kate answered miserably.

Lee turned the nose of the yacht towards the exit of the Broad, and in silence they made their way back up the creek.

'I'll just pop up to the house to say goodbye to your mother,' Kate said when they reached the staithe, 'then I'll get back home.'

Lee looked at her downcast face. 'Would it make things any easier for you if I went to see your father and apologized?'

'For what? No, thanks, I'm quite sure it wouldn't,' she told him. 'I should have told him where I was coming, but he didn't ask me, so I—'

Lee gave her a startled glance. 'You didn't tell him you were having tea here? Does he object to your friendship with my mother?'

'He doesn't know.'

'Doesn't know? But that's very wrong of you. Don't you tell your father who your friends are?'

'Father will have to learn that I'm no longer a child —indeed that I haven't been for some years now,' she flashed back, stung into saying the wrong thing. It was not her father who treated her like a child, it was Lee— Lee—

She ran ahead of him up to the house and found Jane in the kitchen.

'Is something wrong?' Jane asked quickly, glancing at her face.

Kate shook her head. She didn't want to talk now. 'No, it's just that I—have to go. Thank you so much for asking me and—showing me the house. It's—it's been lovely.'

' Not at all—' Jane murmured uncertainly.

On a sudden impulse Kate kissed her cheek, then turned and went out swiftly. Lee was still standing by the water's edge. Kate compressed her lips and passed him to get into her boat without a word. She was too hurt and angry to trust herself to speak.

' I'm sorry you're so upset,' he said as he let go her mooring rope for her.

' It's nothing. Goodbye—and thanks,' she forced herself to answer.

It would take too long to explain, even if she wanted to, fully. How could she say that she was in love with him and yet most of the time he treated her as if she were not quite grown up, and that the rest of the time he was critical of her? She was not upset about her father, not in the way he thought. She was certainly not afraid of him. But she was worried about him, sorry she had angered him and sorry she had not made a point of telling him she was having tea with Mrs Thornton.

There was no sign of her father at the landing stage. As soon as she had moored her boat Kate hurried inside the house. She found him sitting moodily by the window of the sitting room, deep in thought.

' Father, there you are!'

At the sound of her voice he turned, then rose from his seat and walked towards the door.

' Father, I'm—'

But he silenced her with a quick shake of his head and his gaze brushed over her lightly, rather absently, as he went out of the room without saying a word.

Kate gazed after him, completely at a loss. This was so absolutely unlike her father. He had not looked angry, but not indifferent, either. It was difficult to explain.

Worriedly, she set about preparing their Sunday high tea. What was wrong with him? Was he really so upset at seeing her with Lee, or was there something else?

When tea was ready she called him in and he went upstairs to wash. He sat down at the table without a word, and even Kate's attempts at ordinary conversation were met with the briefest of replies. At last Kate could stand it no longer.

'Father, I'm sorry—'

'For what? I have never dictated nor attempted to dictate to you about your friends or your comings and goings.'

Obviously what he regarded as her secrecy had hurt him. 'I—know you haven't, Father,' she answered quietly. 'But this is rather different.'

He flashed her a fierce glance. 'How different?'

'Well, I— But of course it is. It's not everyone you order off the premises. In fact it's the first time you've ever done so that I'm aware of.'

'And so you're going off to meet this man in secret?'

'No, Father. You've got it all wrong.'

'Oh,' he said slowly. 'Well, I'm glad of that.'

But he sounded sceptical. Kate took a deep breath. 'What I'm sorry about, Father, is not telling you where I was going this afternoon.'

He shrugged, but not from indifference. Kate was sure that he was doing his best not to act the heavy-handed father.

'Well, it is customary in this house,' he said mildly. 'It's a matter of both courtesy and common sense.'

'I know, but on this occasion I—shirked it, I suppose. If you'd asked me I would have told you and in any case—'

'I thought you were merely going for a sail. I had no idea you were going to meet *him*.'

'Father, I wasn't! As a matter of fact, I thought he

was away for the weekend. His mother invited me for tea.'

'His mother? But why, unless—'

'We—we just like each other, that's all, Father. It—it has nothing to do with—the man you—dislike so much.'

Eric Martham raised his head and gazed past her to a point somewhere on the opposite wall. Then he went on with his meal and for a long time he did not speak, then he asked:

'Did you see over the house?'

Relieved that he appeared satisfied and was no longer angry, Kate told him all about the house, describing each room and how Lee and his mother were planning gradually to put the whole place in order.

'Who bought it, actually?' he asked. 'Thornton or his mother?'

'It's—his, really,' she answered, trying to keep her voice casual. 'But when—when Lee gets married she will have a self-contained flat upstairs. There's plenty of room.'

'Is he thinking of getting married?'

'I'm not sure. His mother spoke as if he was.'

'Mm. Somebody from Wymondham, I suppose. That's where they came from, I believe you said. Is there another cup of tea in the pot?'

'Yes, of course.'

He passed his cup, and after that seemed disinclined to talk any more. After tea he wandered outside again, and Kate busied herself with the washing-up and other domestic jobs.

During the afternoon of the following day, Jane Thornton telephoned Kate.

'Lee told me about seeing your father—and how angry he looked,' she said. 'I'm sorry if I made things difficult for you by inviting you here.'

Kate reassured her. 'As a matter of fact, once I'd explained to him, he wasn't really angry. He asked me all about the house. It was silly of me not to tell him before I set off.'

'But he still disapproves of Lee?'

'Well, of his views, I suppose—yes.'

There was a short silence. 'And he doesn't mind your friendship with me?' asked Jane.

'He was a little surprised, but he raised no objection. Why should he? It would be unusual if he did. I've always been perfectly free both in my choice of friends or anything else I wanted to do.'

'I understand, my dear. Well, goodbye for now. I shall be seeing you soon.'

Feeling heavy-hearted, Kate put down the receiver. Clearly her father wouldn't have been very pleased if she had been meeting Lee. But there was no need for him to worry. Lee did not see her in a very favourable light at all, still less a romantic one.

Her father went out after lunch, saying that he was going to see Lance's father. When he returned he asked her to make some tea.

'I want to talk to you, Kate.'

'Yes, all right, Father.'

With something almost akin to foreboding in view of his recent moodiness, she made the tea and took it into the sitting room with some of the small cakes she had made.

'Lance said he'd be coming round this evening,' he told her as she poured the tea.

'Oh, well, that will be nice,' she answered automatically.

She sugared his tea and handed it to him, then passed him a plate and held out the cakes for him to take one of them, waiting for him to say what he wanted to talk about.

He stirred his tea slowly, leaving his cake untouched for a moment or two. Then he said:

'I might as well tell you, Kate, I've—er—entered into a sort of partnership with Jim Faulkner.'

'A partnership?' she echoed. 'But—but, Father, why?'

'Why not? It's another iron in the fire. Besides, it will probably be something for you one day—I hope.'

Kate stared at him. 'Something for me? I don't understand.'

A pained expression distorted his features. 'Kate, must you repeat everything I say like that? It's simple enough. He and I have gone into partnership and bought a small boathire business that Lance is going to manage. Jim was short of capital, so, as you and Lance might one day decide to get married—'

Kate put down her cup with a bang. 'Father, how can you assume that? Lance and I are friends, that's all.'

He gave her a long hard look. 'Lance wants to get married. He's told his father so. Has he asked you yet?'

Kate sighed. 'Yes, he has.'

Eric Martham's look sharpened. 'He has? And you turned him down?'

'I—I don't love him in that way. I'm fond of him, but—'

Her father gave an impatient gesture. 'Love—fond? What's the difference? One is sometimes indistinguishable from the other.'

'Love, Father, is what you felt for Mother, what you felt for each other, and what you still feel for her after all these years,' she told him quietly.

He closed his eyes momentarily, then groaned aloud. 'Oh, Kate, Kate, if only I could make you understand!'

'Understand what, Father? What *is* wrong these

days? Can't you tell me?'

He shook his head swiftly. 'It's nothing. I just want to see you with a—man and a place of your own, that's all.'

'But, Father, I could never leave you to look after yourself.'

He eyed her sternly. 'Now that is just plain nonsense. I'm not having you throwing away a chance of happiness just because of me, do you hear? So don't get the idea that you're going to stay home and look after me for the rest of my life. I shall see that you're all right financially, you don't have to worry about that.'

'I'm not worried about that, not in the least. If I were in love with Lance it would be a different matter, but even then I wouldn't leave you to look after yourself.'

He sipped his tea. 'My dear Kate, have you never heard of housekeepers? As to being in love with Lance —well, there are different kinds of love. Yours is probably the quieter, gentler kind. It doesn't take everyone in quite the same way. It sometimes develops more fully after marriage, when you've lived, worked and planned together for something as your mother and I did. So don't, for goodness' sake, Kate, hold Lance off because of me. You just go ahead and get married as soon as you feel inclined.'

Kate sighed and picked up the teapot. 'I'll go and make some fresh. This must be cold by now.'

She was glad to make her escape. Her father was convinced that she was sacrificing her life's happiness for his sake, and that she was in love with Lance, or could be if she were not restraining herself. If he only knew the truth! If, by some remote chance, by some fantastic miracle, Lee were to ask her to marry him she would do so tomorrow. She would not do so without thought for her father, of course. She would make sure that he was being looked after by someone he liked, visit him every day, do some cooking for him—

She pulled herself up quickly. This was futile kind of thinking. Her father need have no fears.

She made fresh tea and took it in. Her father gave her a questioning look.

'You made off sharply. Been doing some thinking?'

She forced herself to smile. 'Yes, Father, I have. I shall do as you say—go ahead and get married as soon as —well, as soon as I feel inclined, as you said.'

'You can see my point about stronger feelings developing after marriage?' he persisted.

'Oh yes. I'm sure you're right. I—I should think the basic thing is to *like* each other, to be able to enjoy each other's company on an ordinary level, and to have a lot in common. The important things, anyway, like love of the countryside and simple pleasures and not to be violently opposed on politics or religion—'

Relief flooded his face. 'That's my girl! You've got it absolutely right. Pass me another of your marvellous cakes. I'm hungry.'

Obviously what she had said had pleased him a great deal, but Kate felt almost in despair. Up to a point she had believed what she had said. Those things were important to a happy marriage, but one should feel something else, too. One should have so much love that the denial of expression was almost too painful to be borne, that the very thought of going through the rest of one's life apart was like a life without hope, without light, a minute-by-minute longing—

Her father's voice broke into her painful thoughts, and she would have been grateful but for the fact that he was still pursuing the subject of Lance and herself.

'I think you and Lance will enjoy working up that business just as your mother and I did,' he was saying.

'Has—Lance agreed to run it, then?' she asked.

'Why, certainly he has. It's an opportunity of a lifetime.'

'But if the business belongs to you and his father, how—'

He gave a broad smile. 'Ah! Now I'm glad you've mentioned that. It's all been taken care of. Lance will be a working partner, you see. Neither I nor his father will interfere in any way. He will be able to do as he likes, develop it in his own way.'

'Isn't that rather a contradiction, Father? *Do as he likes, develop it in his own way.* Suppose Lance doesn't want to develop the business? Suppose he just wants to jog along as it is, keep the business small, make a modest living?'

He stared at her. 'Of course he'll want to develop it. What a ridiculous way to talk! I don't know what's come over you lately, you seem so contrary.'

'I'm sorry, Father. I don't mean to be,' she said hastily. 'He'll want to make some improvements and build it up, I'm sure.'

But what she was equally sure about was that Lance had not the same ambition for development that his father had, certainly not that her own father possessed in his early days as a boat-owner.

Lance drove up to the house about eight o'clock that evening. Eric Martham purposely left them alone together.

'I suppose your father has told you all about the boatyard they've bought at Thurne?' Lance began in a resigned sort of voice.

She nodded. 'You don't sound exactly overjoyed about it. I take it you've changed your mind about getting away from the Broads?'

'I'd never actually decided. It was just one of those things, a mood, I suppose. Anyway, Father was so set on this new idea of his, and what reason could I give him for wanting to get away that he'd understand?'

'I know. Sometimes it seems that parents don't know a thing. We're the older, wiser ones. You're expected to make something of that boathire business, you know, develop it and all that.'

He shrugged. 'Well, of course, I shall to some extent. It's been badly neglected and allowed to run down. But I shall never get it to the size of yours or ours. They've made me a working partner, did your father tell you?'

She nodded. 'But will it ever be *yours*, Lance? What's going to happen if your ideas and theirs don't match up?'

'Ah! But, there's one other thing. Within three years' time I have the option to buy it at *today's price*. That is, the price at which it was bought by our two fathers. It's written into the agreement.'

He sounded pleased. 'That's what you'd like, is it, Lance? To be able to own your own boathire business?'

'It's nice to be one's own boss, anyway, but when I've collected enough capital to buy it, I shall be satisfied to tick over, if by ticking over I can make a reasonable amount of money to live on. But that I don't say to Father because it simply isn't any use. So, as W.S. Gilbert would say, he is right and I am right and all is right as right can be. There's only one snag,' he added with sudden seriousness.

'And that is?' prompted Kate.

Lance gave a sigh and looked at her with a twisted smile. 'In a word, my dear Kate—you.'

'Me?' she squeaked. 'Now look, Lance, I don't know what Father's been saying to you, but—'

'Kate—' Lance reached for her hand, 'Let me ask you one question, then when you've answered it we can talk some more.'

'All right.'

'Remember, this has nothing to do with what my

father wants or what your father would like. I once asked you to marry me. What would your answer be if I asked you again? You didn't really give me a straight answer before, and I'd like a straight answer. Now.'

Kate squeezed his hand, then let it go and walked a step or so away from him.

'If you want a straight answer now, Lance, it—would have to be no.' She looked at him anxiously, most unwilling to hurt him. There was a lost, downcast look on his face, and her heart smote her. 'Lance, I'm sorry. Really. I daresay we could make a go of it, but that isn't good enough. I'm not in *love* with you as I should be for marriage, and I don't get the impression that you are with me, either. We ought to be—well, frantic about each other, and we're not. As a matter of fact,' she went on, warming up to the subject, 'I think you're more in love with Millie than you are with me.'

Lance's eyes shot wide open. 'With Millie?' he almost shouted. 'Are you crazy? In love with that—that—silly little idiot, chasing after a man old enough to be her father.'

'Don't be ridiculous, Lance. He isn't more than about ten years older than she is.'

'I don't care what you say. He just isn't her type. What she wants is a jolly good spanking!'

Kate looked at his agitated expression, and it suddenly occurred to her that what she had said in jest was actually the truth. He *was* in love with Millie, but almost certainly without realizing it. But if Millie was not in love with him, wouldn't it be the kindest thing to steer him away from the idea?

'I was only joking, Lance, of course. The idea is a bit ludicrous.'

But even as she spoke his whole frame stiffened and he gripped his arms. He turned slowly and looked at her, his eyes staring at her yet not really focusing on her. Then an expression of exquisite pain marred his features.

'You're right, Kate. Heaven help me, you're right. I'm as jealous as hell of Thornton. I'd like to take hold of Millie and shake her. But then I'd like to put my arms around her too, and—kiss her until we were both exhausted. I *am* in love with her, but until now I never realized it. What a *fool* I've been, what a fool!'

He clenched his fists and beat the air in anger against himself. Kate's sympathy went out to him.

He turned and spoke to her. 'Kate, how is it possible I didn't realize it before?'

She shook her head. 'I don't know, Lance, but I'm sure you're not the first person to get his emotions all mixed up. The trouble is, we've all grown up together, as it were. You, me, Millie and the rest. There's practically a brother and sister affection among us. We know each other so well.'

'Do we?' he queried with a show of bitterness. 'There's one thing for sure. I don't know what's got into Millie these days.'

'If—if you're referring to her—friendship with Lee Thornton, Lance—well, it's just somebody new for her, that's all. It probably won't last.'

'If only I could believe that. Kate, what's wrong with me?' he appealed almost in despair.

'There's nothing wrong with you, Lance! You're a thoroughly nice, likeable—'

'I don't want to be just likeable.'

Kate suddenly remembered what Millie had said about Lance, how he was at the beck and call of his father and didn't seem to have a mind of his own.

'Perhaps when she sees you managing your own business she'll sit up and take notice, as it were,' she offered. 'I think she's the sort of girl who wants to feel her man is—well, a little bit larger than life. Besides, Lance, you *have* been seeing a lot of me, haven't you?'

' I suppose so. But she's been behaving very off-hand for some time now.' He frowned and shook his head. ' I honestly thought I was in love with *you*, Kate. How could I have?'

She smiled. ' I'm sure it's not uncommon. You and I have always liked each other and got on well together, and in the early stages people in love *are* often angry with each other or even dislike one another. It's rather difficult to understand.'

' You seem to understand it, anyway.'

She laughed. ' It comes of reading romantic novels.'

' I'll try it some time. By the way, how about coming along to have a look at " my " boatyard, seeing that I'm here? Maybe you'll have some suggestions to make.'

Kate said she'd like to. She called out to her father and told him where she was going. Approval was written all over his face. Kate sighed. He was going to be extremely disappointed when he realized Lance wanted to marry Millie and not herself.

' I hope your father won't feel he's wasted his money, you and me not getting married,' Lance said as he drove off.

' It can't be helped. You can't order people's lives like that. He'll probably regard it as a loan. After all, he'll get his money back, won't he?'

' Providing I make a go of the business.'

' Of course you'll make a go of it. You mustn't let yourself think otherwise. Satisfied customers always come back. Remember that. And they tell their friends.'

' I suppose so. But some of the craft looked awfully scruffy, I thought. I went along there on Saturday morning while most of the boats were in.'

' There you are then, Lance. Your first job will be to

spruce them up a bit—a coat of paint, new curtains.'

Lance flashed a smile at her. 'I'd like to think Millie would have your interest.'

'Try her, Lance,' urged Kate. 'As soon as possible bring her along to see the place, ask her advice, let her know how you feel about her. Perhaps if she knew, she—'

Kate broke off. In her eagerness to see Lance happy she had forgotten that Millie might be genuinely in love with Lee. So might he with her, for that matter, in spite of the contrary impression he gave on the night they all met at the Norwood Rooms.

'It's not as easy as it sounds, Kate.' Lance's quiet voice broke into her thoughts. 'If there's one thing men are afraid of when it comes to women, it's rejection. Millie hasn't been very easy for a little while now, and I'm sure a lot of it is to do with Thornton. You said earlier on that you didn't think it would last, it was just a case of a new face, and I hope to goodness you're right. I—I suppose you wouldn't like to do something for me?'

'You know I will, if I can.'

He hesitated momentarily, then gave her a swift, side-long glance. 'I—suppose you wouldn't sort of—try to get him away from her?'

'Lance!'

He grinned sheepishly. 'It would be in a good cause, and they can't possibly be serious about each other. In fact, I thought he seemed rather smitten with you the other night.'

Kate took a deep breath and closed her eyes momentarily. 'Oh, Lance, you don't know what you're asking. I couldn't. For one thing, it's—not the kind of thing I like doing. I mean—supposing they *were* serious about each other? In any case I wouldn't succeed. You got it all wrong about his being remotely "smitten" with me. I don't believe he even likes me. We just don't agree about things. And you know how it is with him and Father. No, Lance, I'm sorry, but I simply couldn't do it. This is something you'll just have to work out for yourself. Try to show her you're as much of a man and as good a man as he is. Chase her a bit.'

'Well, of course I will. I don't want you to do my courting *for* me. The trouble is—as I've told you—she's so ungetatable.'

'Maybe she won't be if you keep on trying, and if I do get talking to her some time, perhaps I could find out how she does feel about—Lee.' She couldn't bring herself to call him Thornton as Lance and her father did. But the next moment she was telling herself she should have done.

'Why do you call him Lee,' Lance asked, 'if you're not on friendly terms with him?'

'His mother does her shopping at our place. She calls him that, naturally, and I've got it from her.'

'What's she like?' Lance asked curiously.

But by now they had arrived at the boatyard, and Kate answered briefly that she was 'very nice'.

Lance drove through a gate which hung askew and looked as if it would fall to pieces if any attempt was made to close it, and brought the car to a halt on a patch of humpy ground at the side of a boat shed where two or three cars were parked. There was a great deal of litter all around—old and rotting timber, broken life-belts, empty oil drums, decaying ropes and rusty chains.

But what dismayed Kate most of all was the sight of the half burnt-out hull of a cruiser almost on the edge of the quay. To the uninitiated the hulk looked as if it had been recently lifted from the water, but the green slime which overlaid the fire-blackened stumps of timber showed it had spent at least one winter ashore. The sight showed the ultimate in lack of caring. A sunken craft was enough to cause apprehension to hirers, but one which had been destroyed by fire—

She turned to Lance. ' I should think the sight of that is enough to put any holiday-maker right off a Broads holiday for life.'

He agreed, ' To get rid of that will be my first job.'

They got out of the car and looked around. ' There doesn't seem to be anyone about,' Kate said, ' and yet the boat shed is open.'

' Maybe there's somebody in there. It's the easiest thing in the world to play a sort of hide and seek in a boatyard—not see a soul, yet there's somebody in and out of the sheds and things and you just miss them each time.'

But now as they entered the badly-lit interior they could hear voices. Lance called out, and from behind an upturned boat came the foreman of the previous owner, Jeffrey Davies.

' Hello there, Lance. Been having a look around?' As they approached he said a polite good-evening to Kate, and it was then that Lee emerged.

Jeffrey made the unnecessary introduction. ' This is Lance Faulkner who's going to run the place, Mr Thornton. And Kate Martham, his girl-friend. Their parents own two of the biggest fleets hereabouts. Kate, this is—'

' We've already met,' she told him somewhat sharply, not pleased at being referred to as Lance's girl-friend, though she supposed locally that was how she was regarded.

Lee was eyeing her speculatively. Kate could guess at some of the things which were going through his mind, but there was little she could do about it. He spoke to Lance.

' I expect you've got all kinds of ideas for the place? Enlarging, improving?'

'Naturally,' answered Lance curtly.

Lee nodded as if to say, *I thought so*.

'It will be a good opportunity for Lance. Show them what he's made of,' Jeffrey Davies said. 'My boss lost interest in the place a long time ago and says he'll be glad to get out of the rat race.'

'I don't know that it is a rat race,' Kate flashed back. 'And this place certainly needs building up.'

Jeffrey Davies grinned. 'The boss's words, not mine. Anyway, a boatyard like this is just the thing for a couple like you and Lance to get your teeth into.'

The implication was obvious and Kate saw Lee's eyebrows raise just a shade. But before she could answer, Jeffrey spoke again.

'Well, I must be off. Come Saturday it will be all yours, Lance.'

Lee said he must be going too, and strode off ahead of the rest.

'What did he want?' Lance asked of Jeffrey.

'I don't rightly know—except that he said he wanted to buy a half-decker. Anyway, we haven't any to sell. But he's the fellow who put the cat among the pigeons by that article a few weeks ago, isn't he?'

'The same,' Lance answered.

By the time they emerged from the boat shed, Lee was in his car and driving away. Jeffrey locked up and went off on his bicycle.

'Is he staying on as your foreman?' asked Kate.

Lance nodded. 'He's a working foreman, anyway.'

'Have you made any plans yet?' she asked as they got back into the car.

'I don't know whether they're plans or day-dreams. Day-dreams, I think, so far.'

'Tell me about them,' she urged, as thoughts of Lee, ever with her in some degree, were becoming painful as well as more insistent. 'You know this is how Mother and Father started. In a small way. It must have been fun.'

Lance patted her knee. ' I still think you and I should have been getting married. We would have made a marvellous team. Life's very contrary.'

Kate agreed with him in part. It would have been exciting as well as fun to build up a successful, going concern from a small neglected one, in spite of anything Lee might say. But life, as Lance said, was contrary. She was not in love with him nor he with her, and she could hardly offer to work for him in the ordinary way because her father needed her.

' If there's any way I can help in my spare time, Lance, I'll be glad to,' she told him. ' Although I'm sure you'd find Millie helpful too, if only you could get her interested. Ask her if she'd like to come and look at the place.'

' I will—if I can get hold of her. She's so elusive these days.'

' Then write her a letter, you goose.'

She was not at all sure, deep down, that she ought to be encouraging Lance to try to win Millie. Suppose Lee were really in love with her? Swiftly, she urged Lance to tell her his plans or day-dreams.

But it was impossible to fill every waking minute with conversation, and when she was alone the thought of Millie and Lee, or Lee and some other unknown woman, filled her tortured mind. His own mother had spoken of his expected marriage. Altogether, Kate longed for the week-end, particularly Saturday when she would be too busy to have time to think. But she was faced with Wednesday, her day off, and if she did not make good use of it her father would begin to ask questions. So as the weather was still miraculously fine she packed her lunch and took out the *Aerial,* thinking she would try to get as far as Hickling Broad.

There was not much wind for sailing yet, so Kate went along on the engine. At Potter Heigham she moored to lower her mast to go under the low, arched bridge, and while she was moored she drank a cup of coffee she had brought in a flask.

It was pleasant to sit here and watch the fascinating, busy scene. Craft of all kinds and all sizes were moored on each bank on either side of the medieval bridge; some of the larger cruisers, Kate suspected, were waiting for pilots.

The picturesque, stone-built bridge was over seven hundred years old. Some people considered it to be a menace both to road and river users alike, and there was talk of building a new one. But at present it was an important link between the town of Stalham and Burgh St Margaret and the intervening villages, and by river the only way to Horsey Mere and Hickling Broad, two of the largest and most interesting stretches of water in the Broads network. Potter Heigham bridge, however, was so low that many Broads cruisers had to wait until low water in order to navigate it safely, and even then, have an experienced pilot. Some boat-owners made this a rule, because so many boats had been damaged or their canopies torn. Even yachts which were much lower in the water and small craft like Kate's needed to be navigated with care. Added to everything else there were strongly running currents on either side of the bridge, and many an unsuspecting yacht skipper had been pulled almost under the low structure with his mast still up. These consequences could either be disastrous, or 'all in a day's fun', especially for by-standers on the banks or watching from the bridge. But for those concerned the 'fun' would be only in retrospect.

Kate finished her coffee and after deciding that the bridge would take the *Aerial* all right, she started her engine and chugged slowly and carefully under the bridge. Clear away from the current she moored and raised her mast again, and as there was now a little more breeze she also hoisted sail. Passing the row of cheap wooden bungalows squatting impudently along one side of the bank, Kate was reminded sharply of Lee. This was the sort of thing he was fighting against, and he was right. On this point, her father and Lee would agree, she was sure. But she forced herself to stop thinking along these lines. It would be pleasant, of course, to feel that her father and Lee were friends, but it would make no difference to the way Lee regarded her, nor would it do very much to ease the awful pain in her heart.

The going up Candle Dyke was slow, but once in Heigham Sound the breeze was more brisk and it was not long before Kate reached Hickling Broad, cared for by the Norfolk Naturalist Trust. Here, bird life both common and rare thrived in abundance. Swans, herons, wild duck, and if one were patient, the rarer bearded tits and marsh harriers. Kate spent a pleasant half hour sailing and doing a little bird-watching, then decided she was hungry and thought she would have her lunch outside the Pleasure Boat Inn. A cool drink with her sandwiches would be fine.

She brought the *Aerial* within a few yards of the staithe, then quickly lowered her sail to slide gently to a mooring place. Occupied in making the boat fast and tying the sail to prevent it flapping about, she did not notice the couple sitting at one of the tables outside the inn. But as she threaded her way among them to go for her drink she suddenly stopped short to see Lee, and with him one of the most attractive women she had ever seen.

CHAPTER VII

'Hello, Kate.' Lee rose to his feet. 'I didn't expect to see you up here.' He turned to his companion. 'Joanna, this is Kate Martham, daughter of the boat-owner who's our nearest neighbour. Kate—Miss Joanna Wainwright, up from Wymondham for the day.'

The other woman was impeccably dressed, making Kate aware at once of her faded jeans and sweater. She was obviously near Lee's own age, and there was no doubt whatever in Kate's mind that this was the woman about whom Mrs Thornton had been hinting as Lee's future wife.

She remembered her manners sufficiently to say, 'How do you do?' and to smile.

Kate received a charming but speculative smile in return.

'Hello, Kate. Lee doesn't know it, but I've been hearing quite a lot about you.' Her voice was low and husky.

'From Mrs Thornton?' queried Kate.

'That's right. And believe me, it was all good.'

Kate felt she was being patronized by both of them. Why couldn't Lee have introduced her simply as Kate Martham instead of her father's daughter as if she were a child? He hadn't said: 'This is Joanna Wainwright, daughter of so-and-so.' But she was determined to be dignified.

She smiled faintly. 'That was very kind of Mrs Thornton. I must drop in and see her again quite soon. Will you excuse me now?'

She strode off into the inn, a mixture of emotions. This mature, attractive woman was obviously far more suited to Lee than either Millie or herself. Was she the one with whom Lance had seen him? It seemed very likely, and she would hardly come from Wymondham, especially for the day, if she were not on terms of intimate friendship with him. She felt a hand on her arm and spun round to see Lee.

' Kate, why did you rush off so quickly? I could have got a drink for you.'

Taut as a violin string her eyes blazed angrily. ' I'm quite capable of getting my own drink, thanks.'

She gave her order to the man who approached at the other side of the counter, and stood there, not looking at Lee, afraid that her anger might turn into tears any minute. And what would be the good of that? she asked herself raggedly.

' Why are you so angry?' Lee said in her ear. ' What have I done now?'

There was a soft, teasing note in his voice, as though he were talking to a slightly rebellious younger sister.

Kate compressed her lips and took a deep breath. ' Lee, will you please leave me *alone!*' she ground out.

He shrugged as if despairing of her. ' All right,' he said, and turned and left her.

Being in a public place helped Kate to get a hold on herself. She paid for her drink and stayed where she was sipping at it. A few minutes later she heard an engine starting up, and when she strolled across to the window she saw Lee and his companion moving away from the staithe in his launch.

With a heavy heart, Kate took the rest of her drink outside and ate some of her sandwiches.

It took her quite a long time to get home. The wind was variable, but against her most of the time causing her to have to tack her zig-zag way along. She could have started her engine, but she did not have the heart, so kept doggedly on with the vague idea that the more her hands, eyes and mind were occupied the less she would dwell on Lee. But she was like a person on a suspended sentence.

When at last she arrived home with barely enough wind to keep her moving, she was surprised to see Jane Thornton and her father standing together on the landing stage talking. As she drew near, her father moved forward to take her mooring rope.

'You been out all day on your own, girlie?'

He hadn't called her that for a long time, and Kate found it niggled her. Why did everyone insist on treating her as if she were sixteen instead of twenty-two?

What's all this girlie business? she was tempted to ask, but she counted to ten.

'It's good to be alone sometimes, Father,' she answered, then turned to greet Jane, wondering how long she had been there, and what kind of conversation she and her father had been having.

'Lee said he'd seen you up on Hickling Broad at lunch time,' Jane said.

'That's right.' Kate glanced at her father expecting to see some reaction to the mention of Lee's name, but to her surprise he showed none at all. His expression, if anything, was benign—owing to Jane's presence, no doubt, she concluded. Her father was nothing if not courteous towards women.

'I came to see when you're coming to have tea with me again,' Jane Thornton said.

'That's very kind of you.'

Jane gave her a puzzled look. 'What about Sunday, then? I know Saturday is your busy day.'

But in her present state of mind, Kate did not think she could face being in Lee's company, and she could hardly say, *I'll come if Lee isn't going to be there.* Besides—

'I'm sorry, Mrs Thornton, but I've more or less promised to give Lance a hand with the new boatyard.

I do hope you don't mind. I'd love to come another time.'

Eric Martham beamed. He turned to Jane and began to tell her about the new enterprise and what a wonderful opportunity it would be for Lance and so on.

'Takes me back to the time when my wife and I first started,' he mused.

'Would you like to turn back the clock?' Jane queried.

Eric thrust his hands into his pockets and gazed out across the Broad.

'For some things, yes. But I'm getting too old for fresh beginnings.'

'Too old?' Jane laughed. 'Why, you're still young. But of course it depends on what sort of beginning, doesn't it?'

Kate listened only vaguely to their conversation. She was to enclosed in her own unhappy world to be wholeheartedly a part of theirs. She wondered how long they were going to go on making what seemed no more than polite conversation, and whether it would look rude if she left them and went into the house when Jane said:

'Well, I'd best be going. Kate, do drop in any time, won't you? You're always welcome.'

Kate and her father helped her to get away, then walked slowly to the house together.

'A very nice woman, that,' Eric Martham said reflectively. 'Pity that son of hers has got such gimcracked ideas.'

Kate made no answer. What was there she could say that would not start a discussion or argument? She could only agree with him about Jane. Her father looked at her.

'What happened to Lance today, then?'

'I expect he's busy at the boatyard. He won't have so much time for taking day's off from now on.'

'True. I was glad to hear you say you were going to give him a hand on Sunday. Has he got any plans yet?'

Kate told him about some of the ideas Lance had, wondering at the same time how she could make him understand, without upsetting him, that she was not going to marry Lance.

Towards the end of the week the fine weather broke. The holiday-makers stepping off the boats on Saturday morning looked smug after their week of almost un-broken sunshine, congratulating themselves as though the fine weather had been in some way due to their own cleverness in choosing that particular week. Those taking over the boats in the afternoon looked up at the sky resentfully, though Kate knew from past experience that, whatever the weather, they would emerge from their floating hotels a week later regretfully, and looking far more relaxed than when they set out.

By Sunday the rain was pouring down. After lunch Kate sat at her bedroom window and looked out over the water, the lancing rain making a multitude of small circles. What was she going to do with her life? How could she bear it if Lee married the woman she had met at the Pleasure Boat and lived here, at Thornton Hall, so near? How long did it take for a love as strong as hers to fade? She supposed it must, sooner or later, but with her whole heart she rejected the idea. She would always love Lee. She simply could not contemplate the rest of her life in which he had no part. But yet again, she tried to tell herself that she would simply *have* to put him out of her mind if he was going to marry some-one else. In any event he had no special regard for her-self, and it was most unlikely that he would ever ask her to marry him, even if there was no other woman left in the world.

She rose swiftly. What was the use of sitting here moping? She might just as well pop over to Lance's boatyard and see how he was getting along. She was more or less bound to, anyway, after what she had said, otherwise her father would think it odd.

She wondered whether Lance had written to Millie and on impulse she dialled Millie's number.

'I suppose you've heard about Lance's new boatyard?' she began.

'Yes, I've heard,' came the non-committal answer.

'I'm—er—just popping over there to see how he's getting on. How about coming with me? I could pick you up in about five minutes.'

'I don't think so, thanks.'

'Why not? Oh, come on, Millie,' Kate pleaded. 'Lance will be awfully pleased to see you.'

There was a slight pause. Then Millie said tartly: 'I don't get it. Why are both you and Lance so eager for me to see his place?'

'Has Lance asked you, then?'

'I had a letter from him yesterday. I don't know why this sudden concern about me. What's the big idea?'

For a moment Kate scarcely knew what to say. Obviously Millie was going to be difficult. It was not going to be easy to win her over. Though Lance had discovered he was in love with her, Millie's own feelings were only supposition.

'I—don't know what you mean,' she answered. 'We're all friends, aren't we? Surely you can show some interest in what Lance is trying to achieve? He needs all the encouragement he can get.'

'I'd have thought he could get as much as he needed from you.' There was a pause then Millie said, 'Actually, I'm expecting a call from Lee. But Mother can take it if Lance is all that keen to show off his new toy.'

Kate held a sharp retort on Lance's behalf in check. She arranged to pick her up, then rang off. She had no idea Millie could be so acid. But the phrase which nagged her the most was: *I'm expecting a call from Lee*. Why should Lee ring Millie? He wouldn't be seeing both Millie and Joanna Wainwright at the same time, surely? Not if he was engaged, at any rate. Kate simply did not know what to make of Lee. Against her will she was beginning to believe that the reputation which had preceded Lee's arrival in the Broadland area was only too true.

As soon as Millie stepped into the car Kate sensed a kind of defensiveness in her attitude.

' I suppose you've already seen over the place?' she asked almost accusingly.

' Well, yes. I expect you know it. It's—'

' Yes, I know. And the idea is that Lance shall run it, make it pay and in time buy it?'

Kate nodded, wondering exactly how much Lance had told her in his letter. Had he told her, for instance, that Kate's father was a partner?

' And I'm sure he will, too. Make it pay, I mean,' she assured the other girl.

Millie grunted, ' It remains to be seen, doesn't it?'

Kate felt a shimmer of irritation. ' Why are you so disparaging—one might almost say contemptuous—of Lance?' she demanded.

' Because he's such a '' yes-man ''. I suppose it was his father's idea that he should try and make something of the Harrisons' down-at-heel place?'

' It was and it wasn't. Lance has wanted to branch out on his own for some time.'

' Then why didn't he?'

' For obvious reasons. He hadn't the capital.'

' So all it means is, his father actually owns the place and Lance is acting as manager.'

Kate sent up a silent prayer for patience. 'No. Lance is a working partner.'

'Really?' Millie said in a disinterested tone.

Kate stopped the car and turned to the other girl. 'Look, Millie, if you're going to keep up this attitude, there's very little point in your coming.'

Millie shrugged. 'I didn't want to in the first place, did I?'

At this point Kate's patience finally expired. 'For heaven's sake, Millie, what's the matter with you?' she exploded. 'Why must you be so mean towards Lance?'

Millie stared at Kate for a moment, her eyes dilated, her mouth set in an angry line. Then suddenly she seemed to crumple. She wrested her gaze from Kate's. 'Oh, all right,' she muttered, 'you win. Though goodness knows why he wants two of us dancing attendance on him.'

Kate started the car again. 'He doesn't. He wants your interest and my practical help. Your help too, if you've any suggestions to make.'

Millie gave Kate a curious, sidelong glance. 'Have you and Lance been talking about me?'

Kate knew that evasions would be useless, though she couldn't betray Lance's confidence. 'We *were* talking about you the other day, as a matter of fact. He was saying how he'd like you to see his new place.'

'But why me?'

'Why not?' Kate countered swiftly. 'We're all friends, aren't we?'

Millie said no more. She sat slumped in the car, and Kate couldn't help wondering what was going through her mind. She was not very happy about something. Could it be anything to do with Lee? Suddenly she felt she must know whether he had rung Millie or not.

'By the way, did Lee ring you?' she asked, keeping her voice as casual as she could.

Millie started, as if she had been deep in thought, and Kate had to repeat the question.

'Oh yes,' Millie answered, 'he rang. Wants to see me tomorrow evening. He couldn't make it tonight. He and his mother have got some people coming over from Wymondham.'

Kate gripped the steering wheel fiercely. Joanna Wainwright today, Millie tomorrow. *Oh, Lee, Lee!*

She was glad when they arrived at the boatyard. Lance was not surprised to see Kate, but his eyes widened at the sight of Millie.

'You've come! This is great. Sorry it's such foul weather. I'm just going through the books in the office. It's not much of a place really. But come on, we can have a cuppa if you don't mind roughing it.'

'Since when did either of us mind roughing it?' laughed Kate.

But deep in her heart she was not laughing. She was thinking of Lee, her mind in a state of confusion as to the kind of man he really was, yet loving him and longing to mean something to him.

Lance was fussing about, peering into the kettle to see whether there was enough water in, chattering about what he was going to do with the office, fiddling about with the teapot.

'Here, give it to me,' said Millie. 'You're like a man with no hands.'

It sounded quite hopeful. Kate wondered whether she should make some excuse to leave them together. Later, perhaps, when they had drunk the tea Millie was making.

Lance went on talking, addressing most of his remarks to Millie.

'Day boats are the thing, Millie, don't you think? Motor launches with good substantial awnings in case of showers. Perhaps your father could build some for me.'

'Have you got any capital?'

'Enough to be going on with. I shall plough most of the profits from the weekly hire craft back into the business. If—if I do well, I shall build a house or bungalow close by. There's plenty of space on the other side of the staithe where those trees are.'

Kate felt he was treading on rather dangerous ground unless he made it clear that it was not herself he wanted to marry. She was framing words to this effect when the telephone rang.

'What, business on a wet Sunday?' murmured Lance as he picked up the receiver. But after a few minutes he handed the instrument to Millie. 'It's for you. Some bloke or other. I didn't ask who it was and he didn't say.'

Millie took the receiver from him, a startled look on her face.

'Yes?' she queried rather cautiously. Then: 'Oh! Oh, hello, Lee. Yes. Yes, that's right.' A pause. 'Well, I—I can't, you see. I'm—not alone.' Another pause. 'Yes, yes, I'll do that. Goodbye, Lee,' she said sweetly, then rang off.

'A very illuminating conversation,' Lance said in a tight voice.

Millie gave a smug little smile and Kate could have hit her. 'That was Lee Thornton,' she said unnecessarily.

'We gathered that,' said Kate. 'I thought you said he'd rung you earlier?'

'So what? He's just rung again, hasn't he? Sorry, folks, I have to go. Do you mind running me back, Kate?' she asked sweetly. 'I can't very well walk back, can I?'

Kate exchanged a glance with Lance and slid off the desk where she had been sitting.

'Be seeing you, Lance. I won't come back, if you don't mind. Give me a ring if there's anything I can do. In any case, I'll probably take a run over on Wednesday just to see how you're getting on.'

The afternoon was not turning out as planned, and that was the sort of thing she hadn't wanted to say in front of Millie, but Lance was still her friend, and she couldn't bear the hurt look in his eyes and the disappointment written on his face.

' 'Bye, Lance,' Millie said casually, ' and the best of luck. See you around.'

' That didn't work out very well, did it?' Kate murmured to Lance as Millie ran through the rain to the car.

He shook his head gloomily. ' It seems pretty hopeless.'

She put a hand on his arm. ' Don't give up, Lance. Not so soon. Millie isn't the only woman in Lee Thornton's life. I saw him with one. She was a much older, very good-looking woman. Maybe it will all turn out right in the end.'

How easy it was to give advice to other people, advice which you could well take yourself. Kate joined Millie and started up the engine.

' A touching little scene,' Millie said mockingly as Kate reversed to leave the boatyard behind. ' " Goodbye, Lance dear, see you on Wednesday." Why Wednesday? That's a long way away, isn't it?'

Kate took a deep breath, but did not answer. Millie had changed from what she used to be. Kate was seriously beginning to wonder whether she were not doing a disservice to Lance by trying to influence Millie on his behalf. It looked as though he would be far more hurt than he deserved.

Without saying another word Kate dropped Millie off at her home and drove away in the direction of Norwich. If she went back home straight away her father would ask questions—why was she home early, where was Lance, why wasn't she spending the rest of the evening with him—and though she realized he would have to know the truth some time, she was not sure that this was the time. She had already tried to tell him, but he simply was not ready to accept it. Perhaps it would be better if he came to realize gradually that there was no possibility of Lance and she ever marrying. If she told him so now, he would only argue that no one could possibly see into the future, that she could never tell what might happen a few months or years hence.

She drove out to Blickling Hall, admired the beautiful furnishings and the antique furniture, and thought immediately of Lee and Thornton Hall. She had tea at Itteringham Mill and dwelt on the afternoon Lee and herself had sat outside and had tea together in the warm sunshine. From Blickling she drove up to Sheringham, then followed the coast road to Sea Palling and so back home. As she had hoped, her father was out and she left his supper on a tray and went upstairs to bed.

The weather remained unsettled for a number of days. Brilliant sunshine alternating with squally showers resulting in stories of boats breaking free of their moorings in the middle of the night, craft getting into difficulties on Breydon Water, and in one case reports of the bowsprit of a yacht crashing clean through the windows of a cruiser, though none of these incidents involved the Martham fleet.

By midday on Wednesday, however, the wind had lessened and skies were clear. Feeling restless indoors, Kate pushed off in the *Aerial* for a sail after lunch. Passing the entrance to the Thornton creek, she realized she had not seen or heard from Mrs Thornton for a whole week. Kate felt it unlikely that Jane had taken offence by her not accepting her invitation to tea the last time she had seen her, but it could be that she was not well or something.

Feeling suddenly conscience-stricken, Kate turned the

Aerial about. She would drop in as Jane had suggested. Lee would be out at his work and so there would be no danger of encountering him.

The water level in the creek was high after the rain and here and there floated blown-down small branches and twigs. The wind was in just the right direction, and within a few minutes Kate had reached the bottom of Thornton House garden. As she made the half-decker fast and walked across the lawn to the house, her heart-beat quickened, as if she expected any minute to see Lee himself come out of the house.

Actually, it seemed so quiet everywhere that Kate was beginning to wonder whether Jane was out. She peered through the French windows which were shut and was about to try knocking on a small door which had not been in use last time she had been here, but the door opened and Lee stood there. Kate's heart gave a great leap.

' Hello,' Lee said without smiling.

' Oh, hello,' she answered breathlessly. ' I didn't expect to see you.'

' I do happen to live here,' he reminded her with a slight lift of his dark brows. ' I suppose you dropped in to see Mother?'

Kate nodded. ' She's not ill, is she? I haven't seen her for about a week now.' Then she added, in case he should get the wrong idea: ' I thought you'd be out.'

' Oh, you did? Well, Mother is away. She was called suddenly to *her* mother, who is ill,' he told her.

' Oh, I see.'

She knew she should simply have said good afternoon and turned and walked away again, but now she was here and he was here too, she wanted to linger. She had quite forgotten for the moment that the last time they had met she had asked him to go away and leave her alone.

He eyed her questioningly. 'Would you like to come in for a minute now that you're here? Or are you in a hurry to get away since you've discovered I'm at home?'

Her pride came to her assistance. 'I don't mind one way or the other. It's normal for a man to be out at work, that's all. Apart from that—'

He smiled then. 'Well, come in, anyhow. I was just thinking of putting the kettle on.'

'Have you been fending for yourself while your mother's been away?' she asked as he led the way into the kitchen.

'Yes—why? Would you have come and looked after me if you'd known?' he teased.

But Kate was not sure how to take him, or how he regarded her, and teasing was one of those things which had a variety of meanings. At the present moment she wanted him to treat her seriously. She wanted to get close to him, to mean something to him.

'I might—if I'd known,' she answered uncertainly. 'But it looks as though you can manage perfectly well on your own,' she added as he deftly dropped the lid on the electric kettle and set the teapot near at hand.

'Ah! But a house is not complete without a woman. It's the old saying in reverse.'

'What old saying?'

'You must have heard it. Something about there being no luck about the house when the good man is away. Well, there's no charm about a house when the " good woman " is away. A house is a house, but a home needs at least two people—a man and a woman.'

'A husband and wife?'

There was a momentary silence. 'If possible,' he said lightly. 'Would you like to get out some cakes and things? They're in the tins over there. And if you'd like some bread and butter—'

She set out a variety of cakes. Some of the smaller

139

ones were quite fresh, and she could not help wondering who had made them. The fruit cake, of course, could have been made by Jane before she left.

'Have you any idea when your mother will be back?' she asked him.

'In a day or two, I think. Gran is improving. She's not so old really. A mere sixty-eight. Why?' he quizzed. 'Thinking of baking me some scones?'

Swiftly into her mind came the retort: *Why don't you ask Millie or Joanna Wainwright?* And equally swiftly came the thought that this was his stock-in-trade, no doubt. This gentle raillery, this teasing. She steeled herself against him and answered casually:

'I might.'

'Might?' he queried, dropping the teapot lid on with a plop. 'A man might starve.'

'And it might do a man good,' she retorted.

His eyes widened comically. 'Kate! I had no idea you could be so cruel.' He picked up the tea tray. 'Well, I shall not starve this afternoon, at any rate. Come on, let's go into my study.'

Kate followed him, carrying the cakes and feeling almost as though she were being admitted into a holy of holies. Lee cleared a low table of papers and they set down the tea things.

'Shall I be mother, as they say?' she asked.

His teasing mood was catching, and she was glad that she was beginning to match his lightness with her own.

'By all means,' he answered.

She poured out the tea and cut the fruit cake, finding a singularly sweet pleasure in the small tasks and, this done, in just sitting there with him. After a minute or two she glanced around. His waste-paper basket was brimming over, his desk littered with papers and books.

'Do you do a lot of work here?' she asked.

'I do most of it here—when I'm not being consulted

about something. This is my " place of work ", my office.'

'Oh, I see.' She glanced at the half-used sheet of paper in the typewriter.

'And what are you writing now—one of your provocative articles?'

It was meant to be light-hearted, but as soon as she had asked the question she wished she hadn't. His face became serious.

'It's almost impossible not to be provocative,' he answered. 'Whatever I say on the subject of the Broads it's bound to upset people with a commercial interest. I'm on the side of the ordinary man and woman—and child—who lives in the country or comes for a day out or a holiday and find they can't get near the riverside for a picnic, or to fish, for Flats Afloat and whacking great cruisers, who can't sail a small boat in peace for those great lumbering things which resemble nothing more than floating bungalows.'

He paused for breath. Kate knew to which cruisers he was referring. They were like great, squat white whales which could take up a good half width of the river. Inside, they were the last word in luxury. A far cry from what was envisaged as 'messing about in boats'. They were monstrosities which many people considered out of place on the winding waterways of Norfolk and Suffolk. As to the Flats Afloat or houseboats such as her father had—

'What I would like to see,' Lee's voice came again, ' is what hundreds of other people would like to see. And that is Broadland being re-established as the—the oasis of serene beauty it used to be.'

'You mean no hire craft at all?'

'No, of course I don't mean that. What I do mean is a limit put on the size of craft, a limit on the number of cruisers in any one fleet. In fact a much stricter control all round for the ultimate good of everyone. I'd certainly ban the mooring of houseboats on the banks of the open rivers. They spoil the whole country appearance, the whole beauty of the rivers. One or two boats quietly moored is a different matter, but those long lines of gaudy houseboats—'

It was impossible for Kate not to agree with him. At the same time she could not help wishing that he did not feel quite so strongly about it all.

'Lee, don't you think you're rather overstating the case?' she said in a troubled voice. 'Isn't it good that so many people want to come to such a lovely spot for a holiday? And they have to be accommodated somehow.'

He shook his head. 'Unless you want to spoil the Broads completely you simply must call a halt to this trend for more and more, and bigger and bigger craft and increased moored accommodation. Already some people are saying that the Broads are too crowded and are staying away. Once you had nature and country-lovers coming to the area. Soon you'll be getting vandals and people who like noise and leave litter. There's already talk of a " litter barge ". At one time such a thing simply would not have been necessary.'

There was no arguing with him. It was all so true. She began to think how much nicer even Cocksfoot Broad would look without the houseboats. That wild, elusive beauty of the rivers and Broads really was in danger of disappearing. But with her father in mind and his and Lee's conflicting views, the thought afforded her little comfort.

Lee eyed her worried face. ' I'm sorry, Kate. That's the worst of feeling strongly about a subject. One is apt to go on a bit. Whatever your own views are on all this—and I think they're moderate—it can't be easy for you with your father and Lance in the boathire business.'

He was being kind and remembering his duty as host. 'I don't really think Father wants to develop any more. And in going into partnership with Lance's father he was just thinking of me. Lance feels he has to make something of that neglected business, naturally, and of course he has plans for adding more craft to the small fleet as well as doing up the existing boats. But he hasn't the same driving ambition that his father has, and he's thinking more on the lines of day boats rather than big cruisers.'

She was aware than she sounded apologetic, and as though she were seeking his approval, but she had been almost speaking her thoughts aloud. She had recognized the truth in what Lee had been saying and did not want to be a part of despoiling elements.

But Lee smiled and patted her shoulder as if she were a child to be consoled and approved of.

'With you to help and advise him I'm sure Lance will do very well.'

Kate did not answer. Obviously he thought she was going to marry Lance. And the idea meant nothing to him. Why should it? she asked herself in despair. She put down her cup with the idea of leaving and glancing up caught a very odd look on Lee's face.

'Anything wrong?' she asked.

He shook his head swiftly. 'No, no. Just one of my more solemn expressions, I expect.'

She rose. 'Thanks for the tea, but I really must be going.'

He said, 'Must you?' politely, but rose with her and walked her to the water's edge. He spoke little except to comment on the weather, but as she let go her bow rope he said suddenly:

'Kate, would you do me a favour?'

She gave him a surprised look. 'Why, certainly, if I can.'

'Will you take pity on me and have dinner with me tonight? Out, I mean—and if you think Lance wouldn't mind.'

For a moment she did not know how to answer him. Why was he asking her? His 'take pity on me' was only a figure of speech, of course.

'I don't think Lance would mind in the least,' she said.

'Then you will? Good. I hate dining out alone and my bachelor life is beginning to pall. I'll call for you at seven, if that's all right.'

'Yes, all right.'

He gave her a push off and the *Aerial* glided smoothly down towards the entrance of the creek. At first, as she steered towards the small gap and turned into the open river, Kate scarcely knew how she felt about Lee's invitation, but gradually a feeling of elation took possession of her. She was going to see Lee, she was going to spend a whole evening with him. Rights, wrongs or his motives did not matter in the least. Nothing mattered in the whole wide world.

CHAPTER VIII

For half an hour or so Kate sailed, the brisk wind filling the lugsail until it strained against the wire stays and sent the craft fairly racing along, the water laughing and gurgling as it lapped the sides of the *Aerial*. Added to the elation in her heart, the excitement and exhilaration was tremendous. The sky was blue, no clouds menaced the sun, everything was fresh, beautiful, and gloriously happy.

What should she wear tonight? Something to make her look older, more sophisticated or the misty blue dress Lee had said matched her eyes? Yes, she decided happily, that was what she'd wear. The misty blue. And what would they talk about? she wondered. Not the Broads again. Oh, not the Broads. Something more —personal and intimate.

She was so immersed in her thoughts she did not realize how far she had sailed and was horrified when she glanced at her watch and saw how late it was. She had barely two hours to get back home, prepare a meal for her father and be ready when Lee called at seven. She turned the *Aerial* about, hoping it would not be necessary to start her engine, which she hated. But by sailing close hauled in some places and tacking in others she made fair headway and was home by a quarter to six.

Her father was waiting on the quayside, and she could not help thinking how lonely he looked. He ought to get married again, she thought. He needed a wife now, perhaps more than ever. If only he did not dwell so much in the past! He needed to marry again for the close companionship a marriage could bring.

'Had a good sail, Katie?' he asked as he took a mooring rope from her and made it fast.

'Wonderful, Father. Simply wonderful,' she answered, unaware of the sparkle in her eyes, the radiant expression on her face.

It did not escape her father. 'Kate, you look so much like your mother sometimes, it hurts.'

'Daddy—'

She put her arm around his waist, and swiftly, his came about her shoulders as together they walked towards the house.

But a moment later Kate's mind was troubled and disturbed about two things. Were she and her father in danger of clinging together too much, influenced by the memory of her mother? And second, what would his reaction be to her going out to dinner with Lee? She almost dreaded his next question which came swiftly.

'You going off out tonight?'

'Er—yes, Father. I'm going out to dinner.'

'Out to dinner? Well, in that case don't worry about a meal for me. I'll go along to the Wherry and have "a pie and a pint". You won't want to eat now if you're having a meal out and you haven't left yourself much time to get ready. Enjoy yourself.'

As they entered the house he gave her a hug and went into his study.

Kate mounted the stairs to her room feeling like a child who had been patted absentmindedly on the head, then had a door closed gently but decidedly in her face. Yet at the same time she was relieved that he had not asked her if she were going out with Lance, but merely assumed it. She sighed. When were their lives going to be normal again?

As she peeled off her sweater she heard her father's heavy tread on the stairs. A few minutes later he went into the bathroom. If she called out and told him now that she was going out to dinner with Lee it would appear that she was giving the matter too much importance. She would tell him when it seemed natural—either when she came in tonight or in the morning at breakfast.

When he came out of the bathroom she went in, and she was only just stepping out when he called out to her that he was going and not to wait up for him if she was in first. She answered him, then with a sudden, awful feeling of guilt she reached behind the door for a bathrobe. She must tell him before he went. But before she could struggle into it, he was down the stairs, and when she called after him he did not hear her. Kate sighed again. Oh well, perhaps she was making too much fuss.

She took considerable pains with her hair, brushing it to a burnished finish, almost wishing she had a hairpiece after all so that she could have had ringlets down the back. But by the time she stepped into her dress, all her worries and misgivings vanished and she wanted to dance and sing.

When Lee called for her she had the satisfaction of seeing his eyebrows raise at the sight of her.

'Wow! I didn't realize I was taking out a duchess,' he said admiringly. 'I'm flattered.'

She lifted her chin. 'There's no need to be,' she told him, then she gave a mischievous smile. 'I don't wear jeans and sweaters *quite* all the time.'

'I didn't suppose for a moment that you did,' he retorted lightly. 'But I'm so glad I've given my car a doing over in your honour.'

With great ceremony he helped her into his car, and she sat back, determined to make this an evening to cherish. It was undoubtedly going to be all she would have.

He took her to a country club she knew well. It overlooked a staithe and had a small area for dancing. Kate had been here often with Lance, and sometimes with a party.

'Have you been here many times before?' Kate asked him.

'A couple of times. And you?'

She wondered briefly who had been with him on those two occasions, Millie, Joanna Wainwright or the woman with whom Lance had seen him? But she put an end to such thoughts firmly. She had promised herself to enjoy the evening. It might not be a bad notion to try a little flirting herself.

She gave a slow smile. 'I've been here fairly often, but never with a more handsome or distinguished-looking man.'

His eyes opened wide. 'Well! Flattery, eh? I can see this is going to be quite an evening.'

But contrarily Kate suppressed a faint feeling of uneasiness. She didn't want to flirt with Lee, nor did she want him to flirt with her. She wanted something much, much deeper.

They sat on a high stool and had a pre-dinner drink, then were shown to a table Lee had reserved for them.

'Do you like champagne?' he asked her when the wine list was brought.

'Why, yes, but—'

'Then champagne it shall be,' he announced. 'This is a special occasion. Believe me, it's not every evening one has the privilege of taking a pretty girl in a beautiful blue dress out to dinner.'

She smiled, but she had far rather he had called her 'a beautiful woman' instead of a pretty girl.

The champagne was duly brought, the cork popped and the glasses filled. Lee raised his and smiled at her across the table.

'To you, Kate—your future happiness.'

'And yours,' she echoed in a hollow voice.

Her life's happiness lay with him and him alone.

Across the table Lee's gaze met hers rather solemnly for a moment. She was the first to look away.

The meal was simply delicious—French onion soup, sole, rare steak cooked in wine and a sweet which was a delightful combination of nuts, fruit and cream.

The combination of good food, music and champagne began to have their effect. Kate relaxed and found Lee the most entertaining of companions. At first he talked about places he had visited abroad and Kate thought how wonderful it would be to travel with a man like Lee. A man of the world who knew his way around, knew how to get service and how to enjoy life.

She sighed. 'I'm afraid I haven't been anywhere much. During the summer we're much too busy to take holidays and in the winter—well, one doesn't have the inclination, somehow.'

He nodded. 'Winter holidays are all very well, but getting there can be very tricky. Fog, snow and so on. Still, I would have thought you could get away say in October when you're not so busy.'

She gave a wry smile. 'There always seems to be plenty to do in the boathire business.'

'But surely you *could* get away if you really wanted to?' he persisted. 'It seems altogether wrong to me not to be able to take a break. You're young, yet you haven't "been anywhere much" because of your father's boathire business. Now you're going to marry a young man who has his way to make in another—'

The intensely personal and painful turn of the conversation caught Kate entirely unawares. Everything within her seemed to cringe and the food in her throat felt as if it would choke her. She tried to answer him, but couldn't.

Lee searched her face and frowned. 'Kate, I'm sorry. I shouldn't have said that. Let's dance, shall we?'

She nodded and rose without speaking. The small

149

orchestra were playing an old-fashioned waltz tune. Lee held her close to him and she allowed her forehead to rest on his cheek. She did not know whether he was holding her closely out of dancing habit or flirtatiousness or to emphasize his apology, and she did not greatly care. She drew comfort from the exquisite proximity and savoured every moment.

'Am I forgiven?' he asked at the end of the first portion of the dance.

She nodded. 'You're quite right really. I *should* have made the effort to see something of the world. I realize that now. Tell me, what do you think of package tours?'

It was a safe enough subject and it was one on which Lee knew quite a good deal.

'The greatest advantage of a package tour,' he told her, 'is that it's cheap. Block bookings of coaches, planes and hotels enable the travel companies to do a whole fortnight for what the fare alone would cost if you went under your own steam. Another advantage is that women in particular can go alone without being *on* their own.'

That will be me, Kate thought bleakly. 'Who have you been with when you've been abroad?' she asked.

'Alone occasionally, but Mother, usually,' he told her. Then he grinned, 'And more often than not we've been taken for husband and wife!'

'I'm not surprised. She *is* very young-looking.'

He nodded. 'She's that. And of course we *are* Mr and Mrs, so the mistake easily arises.'

Mr and Mrs. Mr and Mrs Thornton. Kate repeated the words in her brain. Who would be the young Mrs Thornton?

'I'm surprised your mother hasn't married again,' she ventured.

His expression became serious. He nodded. 'It *is*

150

rather surprising. But I think that—like me—she's kind of hard to please. She wants a man as interesting and as intelligent as my father was, and I suppose I've set my sights on a woman as beautiful and charming as my mother.'

Kate's heart almost stopped beating. 'You—haven't found her yet?'

His eyes clouded, but his expression gave away nothing. 'In a way, I have—yes. But there are complications.'

She longed to ask him what kind of complications, but suddenly he switched the conversation back to travel.

But Kate barely listened. She was wondering, with despair in her heart, who this woman was who rated as high as Jane for beauty and charm. It somehow did not fit Millie, but then Millie was probably at her best with Lee. It could most certainly be Miss Wainwright so far as one could judge on sight. By no stretch of imagination could he mean herself. She was certainly not beautiful and practically every time they had met—with the exception of tonight—they had argued or quarrelled.

'Am I boring you, Kate?'

His words penetrated her thoughts sharply. 'Why—why, no, of course not,' she answered in confusion. 'I —I was thinking of something you said, trying to imagine what—it must have been like.'

'Well, you didn't look too happy about it,' he said frankly, and she wished she could hide her feelings a little better or keep her thoughts under stricter control.

After this they danced once or twice, then Lee suggested it was time to leave.

Outside, they lingered for a while beside the staithe. The lights from moored cruisers reflected in the water like liquid gold and a rising moon shed a rippled path of silver on the black surface. Lee's arm went across her shoulders, and Kate steeled herself against taking it as any more than a purely companionable gesture. But when he spoke she realized it was not even that. He was feeling sorry for her.

' Kate, is everything all right between you and Lance? '

' Why? What makes you ask? ' she jerked out.

He gave her shoulders a gentle hug which was at the same time an exquisite joy she wanted to respond to with her whole heart, and a searing pain knowing he meant little by it.

' It's just that you don't seem very happy at times,' he said kindly. ' That day at Hickling Broad in the Pleasure Boat Inn. Every time Lance's name is mentioned—'

She could stand his kindness, his commiserations, his sympathy no longer. She twisted herself free of his arm roughly.

' For goodness' sake, Lee—I don't *want* your sympathy! There's nothing wrong between Lance and me. Nothing. Please take me home.'

' All right,' he snapped.

He drove her home without speaking another word. Kate sat in complete and utter misery. It was her own fault. She had spoilt what could have been a perfectly wonderful evening. Why couldn't she learn to hide her feelings better? She had lived too long in the country where one behaved naturally.

She was glad that the house was in darkness. She simply could not have faced a talk with her father tonight. All she wanted was to get to her room.

Lee stopped the car and sat immobile for a moment. Kate tried to frame words in which to thank him but after her stupid outburst she felt anything she said would sound hypocritical.

' Lee, I'm sorry.' An apology was more appropriate.

' That's all right.' He stopped the engine, then got out of the car and went round to the other side to hand her out. 'Have you got your key?' he asked, glancing up at the darkened windows of the house.

She rummaged in her handbag and found it, then in the light of the moon she looked up into his face, searching for what, she was not quite sure. But his face revealed nothing.

'Goodnight then, Lee, and—thanks for a lovely dinner and everything,' she said hesitantly.

He looked at her without speaking for a moment, then his hands came up to her shoulders. Her heart began to beat madly and her lips framed his name. Then without warning she was in his arms, his lips hard on hers. How long the kiss lasted she had no idea, but to Kate it was a timeless experience in which she was plunged into heights and depths which had no limit.

She became aware of being thrust deliberately from him and heard him say: 'Goodnight, Kate.' Then he was gone. Like someone in a dream she unlocked the door and let herself into the house. The moment of his embrace had been exquisite and she could still feel the pressure of his lips on hers, but deep inside her heart ached. He had not kissed her because he loved her, but only to round off an evening, or out of a sudden impulse. The evening had been a dismal failure.

She dragged herself upstairs, stripped off the blue dress and hung it in the wardrobe, then with the same listlessness went through the motions of preparing for bed. After leaving a note for her father to say she was home she crept between the sheets, too utterly miserable to think, her mind in a state of semi-paralysis. She did not remember going to sleep.

At breakfast the next morning her father eyed her keenly. 'D'ye have a good time last night?'

'Ye—s. We went to the Staithe. They do a very good meal there.'

'Hm—m. And who is "we"?'

She sighed. 'I went with Lee Thornton, not with Lance.'

'I know. I saw Lance at the Wherry. He was with that girl Millie. What's gone wrong between you two, Kate?'

She put her hand to her head and momentarily closed her eyes.

'Father, nothing's gone wrong. I told you, Lance and I are not in love with each other and we're not going to get married.'

She hadn't meant to put it quite so bluntly. She had meant to impress the situation on her father more gradually. But she was edgy and not herself after last night.

Eric Martham's jaw tightened. He gave her an angry look. 'You're quite determined, aren't you, Kate?'

Kate almost despaired. 'Oh, Father, can't you understand? I'm not *determined* about anything. I can't help the way I feel, nor can Lance.'

'But—but you and Lance have been going out together and spending time with each other for—for years!' he said in an exasperated tone. 'So there's no sense in trying to make me believe there's never been anything between you.'

'I'm not "trying to make you believe" anything, Father,' she told him quietly.

He let out a large sigh. 'Well, something's funny somewhere. Lance wanted you to marry him at one time, didn't he? And not so very long ago at that. Moreover, I could have staked my life on it that you were fond of him.'

'Fond of him. That brings us back to square one, Father,' she reminded him.

'Well, that you were "in love" with him, then. You know what I meant all right.'

They were arguing. Kate was uncomfortably aware

of the fact. It was something her father and she had done very little of in the past. Kate made one more attempt to make him understand.'

'Father, I know it must seem odd to you and I'm sorry if you're disappointed in the way things are turning out. But life isn't always that simple.'

'You don't have to tell me about life, Kate,' Eric Martham interposed bitterly.

'All right. Well, it's the same for us, too. For younger people like Lance and me, I mean. Lance thought he wanted to marry me, he thought he was in love with me, but—well, he was mistaken. For my part, I simply wasn't sure. Now, I am. Lance and I are friends and I hope we always will be. But *that's all.*'

Her father eyed her intently. 'In my opinion you young people analyse things a great deal too much. At least, some of you do. Others don't know their own minds five minutes together. So I suppose now Lance is keen on Millie? And what about you and this journalist fellow—Thornton?'

Kate flinched. 'He's—not a journalist, he's a marine consultant.'

'Don't quibble, Kate. He's fond of writing articles, isn't he? And you've not answered my question. Why'd he take you out to dinner last night?'

'I called to see his mother yesterday afternoon, and it so happened that she was away. Lee was at home— I thought he'd be out, actually—but he asked me to stay for a cup of tea, which I did. Then he said he was a bit fed up with having meals alone, so he asked me to have dinner out with him.'

'Is that all?'

'Yes, Father, that is all.'

'Hm,' he grunted in a sceptical tone. But he said no more, and Kate was relieved.

About the middle of the morning, however, when Kate

strolled into the boatyard café for a cup of coffee, her father was glaring down at something in the morning's paper.

' Just take a look at that! ' he exploded as she joined him. ' He's at it again. And that's the sort of man you're hobnobbing with, having tea with and going out to dinner with. I tell you, Kate, he's no friend of either mine or yours—or shouldn't be.'

Kate felt sick and cold. She cast her eyes on the paper her father pushed over to her and caught a glimpse of words like: . . . *limit the number of hirecraft any one firm may own for hire . . . limit the size of boats . . . ban the mooring of houseboats along river banks and put a limit on the number moored on Broads.* All the things he mentioned to her yesterday.

' Who the blazes does the man think he is? ' stormed her father. ' That man had better watch out. One of these dark nights somebody will be jumping him.'

Kate knew that her father was only giving vent to his feelings, and she could not blame him. At the same time she agreed with most of what Lee had said. But the thing which hurt and distressed her most was the fact that the two people she loved so dearly were such worlds apart.

' Well? ' her father demanded as she did not answer.

She pushed the paper back to him. She would have given anything just to walk out and not say anything at all. But that would make her father even more angry. And yet how was she to answer him?

' I know how you feel, Father,' she began. ' But you must admit those latest big cruisers are somewhat beyond the pale—and the rivers would look better without so many houseboats moored along the banks. We've become so accustomed to seeing them there ourselves, I think we've forgotten how much more natural and beautiful the rivers would look without them.'

Eric Martham stared at his daughter as if she had taken leave of her senses.

'Natural? Beautiful? I never heard such poppycock in all my life! There's plenty of natural beauty for miles and miles along the river banks. And what about his—"limit on the number moored on the Broads"? I suppose you agree with that too, do you? Well, why not ring him up and ask him how many he'd like us to have? Then I'll sink the rest.' He rose suddenly and screwing the paper up into a ball he threw it down on to the table and strode outside.

Kate sighed and smoothed out the crumpled newspaper. She didn't seem to be able to avoid crossing her father these days. But it simply would not be right to pretend to agree entirely if she did not mean it.

She read Lee's article more fully and when she reached the end she was more in love with him than ever. He was a man of both ideas and ideals and expressed them fearlessly in a style of prose which was beautiful to read. She went outside and gazed across the Broad. Lee was right. How much nicer it would look uncluttered by their half-dozen houseboats. But they brought in a great deal of money. From aboard the houseboats themselves the view across the Broad was a beautiful expanse of clear water. It was from the other side of the Broad the view was spoilt, and from where she was standing now on the quayside.

'Without those houseboats,' her father said in her ear, 'our income would be down by somewhere around a quarter.'

'Yes, Father, I know.'

He put a hand on her shoulder. 'Sorry I blew my top just now, Katie. I wasn't really mad at you, only at Thornton. I feel he's getting at us. If he had his way the rivers and Broads of Norfolk would be virtually empty. And who does he think helps to keep the waterways and banks beautiful? Without the revenue from the licences of the hirecraft as well as privately owned boats, plus the donations made from the boat-owners' associations, half these rivers would be silted up and unnavigable. They'd be back to nature all right. Right back—but not very beautiful.'

Kate could certainly agree with this. Hundreds of pounds were spent each year on dredging, weeding, repair of the banks and generally keeping the waterways open. It was a truism that there were two sides to every coin. If only people could be persuaded to look!

It was Saturday evening before Kate saw Jane again. ' I came back home last night,' Jane said, ' but I knew you'd be busy earlier on, so I thought I'd wait until you'd be finished. I hear you paid me a visit while I was away.'

' Yes.' Kate asked how Jane's mother was.

' Better, I'm pleased to say. Lee tells me he took you out to dinner.'

Kate nodded. ' I don't know whether it was altogether successful from Lee's point of view.'

' Oh? Why not?'

Kate sighed. ' I don't know really. I always get the feeling that—that Lee regards me as a—a—well, a girl rather than a woman.'

' He *is* quite a bit older than you, isn't he?' Jane pointed out mildly.

' Yes, but—'

' But you'd like him to treat you as though you were older.'

Kate frowned, then shook her head. ' Not really. After all, I'm twenty-two. That's surely woman enough for any man?'

' True. But you think he treats you as if you were younger than you are?'

' Sometimes, but not always, of course. I suppose

158

the truth is, he's used to much older women.'

Jane Thornton smiled and gave Kate's hand a gentle squeeze. 'I wouldn't make too many assumptions if I were you. Lee is not quite himself just now, anyhow, and I'm afraid he's stirring up a regular hornet's nest with those articles of his. Is your father very angry about the latest one?'

'I'm afraid he is, and of course I can see only too clearly his point of view. I wish with my whole heart that they *could* see eye to eye, even though—' Kate broke off. She could hardly say: *Even though Lee isn't in love with me.*

'My dear, I know how you feel. But men are obstinate creatures—even the ones we love. Lee feels he has to keep pegging away at this Broads thing until something is done to control commercialism.'

'And Father feels he's getting at us.'

'He isn't, of course. I'm sure of that,' Jane said swiftly.

'I suppose not. All the same—' Kate broke off as her father called her name.

She swung around, wondering what his reception of Lee's mother would be in view of the article. He stopped short at the sight of her, but any anger he might have felt melted under the warmth of Jane's smile.

'Good evening, Mr Martham.'

He nodded. 'Evening, Mrs Thornton,' he answered, then turning to Kate, 'Lance is on the phone. Wants a word with you.'

She thanked him and asked Jane to excuse her then walked towards the house. A glance behind her just before she entered showed Jane and her father still standing together, and Kate was relieved. After all, it was not Jane's fault that Lee held such strong views in conflict with her father's.

'Hello, Lance,' she said, picking up the telephone.

'Ah, Kate. How are things? Have you just about finished for the day?'

'Just about.'

'Good. Then how about coming round to our place for a bit of a party? Just the old crowd.'

'Oh, Lance, no. I don't feel like a party somehow. Have you asked anyone else yet?' He said he hadn't.

'Then why not let's meet at the Wherry as usual?'

He agreed, though reluctantly, it seemed to Kate, and she wondered why.

'Have you seen Millie since I brought her over last Sunday?' she asked.

He hadn't. He'd rung her once or twice, but, 'I'm not getting anywhere with her at all. I still think she's seeing that Thornton fellow.'

'Well, maybe she'll be at the Wherry,' she consoled him.

She rang off as soon as she could. What was it Jane had said in answer to her remark about Lee being more used to older women? *I wouldn't make too many assumptions, if I were you.*

When she went outside again Jane had gone and Eric Martham was gazing moodily across the Broad. As Kate joined him he gave a heavy sigh.

'What's the matter, Father?' she asked. 'Feeling a bit fed up?'

'Not exactly, Kate, no. It's just that every now and then I wish things were different. It's not too late, I suppose, but—'

He seemed almost to be talking to himself. Kate waited for him to talk further. She had a vague idea of what was troubling him, but could only guess unless he was more explicit. But suddenly he appeared to rouse himself and asked:

'Well, what did Lance want? Anything special?'

'No, only to ask me if I would see him at the Wherry.'

' Are you going?'

' I might—unless you want me here.'

' No, no, you push off any time you want. I'll probably take a run out myself later.'

Partly to please Lance and partly because she knew that if she stayed at home she would start thinking about Lee again, Kate drove along to the Wherry about eight o'clock. The place was filled with the usual boating fraternity—men in great thick sweaters which looked as if they had been knitted on broomsticks, girls in trouser-suits or jeans and sweaters, a preponderance of woolly caps bobbing about and over all an atmosphere of buoyant friendliness and leisure.

Lance was in his usual corner with Tony and David, but of Millie there was no sign.

' She says she might come along later,' Lance said gloomily.

Kate said nothing. She was beginning to lose patience with Millie and with Lance too, for wearing his heart on his sleeve so much.

' Is she still hanging around that Thornton fellow?' queried Tony.

' She's a fool,' David said bluntly. ' Did you see that article of his in the E.D.P. the other day? The man's mad.'

' Oh, please—' implored Kate, ' don't let's talk about that again!'

But she realized only too well that she too was in danger of wearing her heart on her sleeve. In spite of her protest they did discuss the article and its implications for a while. Kate noticed Lance's glance go to the door now and then, and then Millie came in at last and right behind her was Lee. Kate tensed and looked away.

' Christopher, they're coming over here—both of 'em,' muttered Tony. ' I must say he's got a nerve!'

' Right into the lion's den, you might say,' David murmured.

Kate prayed that she would not give herself away. As Millie and Lee approached their table she tried to appear natural. She looked up and smiled. The three young men half rose politely and Lance brought up a chair for Millie.

'Are you going to join us, Lee?' Kate said, not thinking for a moment that he would.

'Thank you,' he said to her astonishment, also to that of the other three, she felt sure.

He found a stool for himself and sat down. Lance's face was dark and Millie did not look any too pleased either. Poised and confident, Lee looked from one to the other.

'I don't think we've met, have we?' he said to David and Tony.

It was Kate who made the introductions. Lance was asking Millie what she would like to drink, but Lee, it seemed, had ordered for himself and Millie on the way in.

With a gleam of mischief in his eyes, Tony said: 'As a matter of fact, we were just talking about you, Mr Thornton.'

'Really? In what connection? If there's anything about me you want to know—'

Kate tried to kick Tony under the table, but from the odd glance she received from Lee, she had kicked the wrong person.

'It's about these articles of yours in the local paper,' Tony went on. 'You know, I think you're up the pole.'

Kate gasped, 'Tony!'

But Lee smiled easily, 'No, Kate, let's hear what everybody's got to say.'

His glance flicked invitingly from one to the other around the table. Kate saw Lance's jaw tighten and suddenly she wished he would stand up to Lee, show Millie what he was made of. She gave his foot a little tap and this time it was right on target.

He gave her a sharp glance, then glared across at Lee. 'All right, if that's the way you want it, Mr Thornton. I think you're more than up the pole. I think you're a downright menace.'

Lee opened his eyes wide. 'Well now, those are strong words. In what way do you think I'm a menace—bearing in mind that we're talking about my articles in the paper on the Broads situation.'

'I'll bear it in mind all right,' Lance retorted. Millie gaped at him, but he simply ignored her. 'I say you're a menace because you're threatening the livelihood of hundreds of people in this area. And I don't mean just the boat-*owners*, the big fellows who own several fleets. I'm talking about the little people. The engineers, the maintenance men, the apprentices, the carpenters, office workers, and the Saturday morning cleaners, middle-aged women mostly, earning a few extra pence to buy themselves some decent clothes. Do you ever stop to think about them?'

There was a moment of silence. Kate saw the dawning of admiration in Millie's eyes at Lance's eloquence. With bated breath Kate waited for Lee's answer, and the others at the table eyed him expectantly.

But nothing, it seemed, could shake Lee's confidence and assurance.

He answered quietly: 'Don't you see, Lance? They are the very people whose livelihood will not be merely threatened, but taken away, *if the present trend is continued*. The Norfolk Broads holiday has become popular *because* it offers peace—a quiet, relaxed, peaceful holiday *away from crowds*. If the river banks are allowed to become lined with houseboats, chalets, shops, restaurants and the like, and it becomes impossible to sail a boat for the number of whacking great cruisers, speed-boats and heaven knows what, then the people who want the sort of holiday on which the trade has been built will stay away. It's as simple as that. The goose which was laying the golden eggs will have been killed. All I'm doing is trying to protect the small boatyard owners like yourself, and the pioneers like Kate's father, as well as all the little people you spoke about. I'm also trying to preserve the natural beauty of the rivers and Broads for lovers of the countryside which include myself. And, I'm sure, all of you.'

Again there was a silence, but this time the small group were impressed. Kate felt there was nothing more to be said. Lee had given the perfect answer. When he had referred to Lance as a boatyard owner she detected a glow of pride both in Lance's eyes and in Millie's. Her own pride was in Lee and she wished her father could have been here. The silence was broken by David, who obviously wanted the argument to continue.

'Well, of course, that's all very well in theory, but how're you going to call a halt? Who's to say—'

'How?' Lee came back swiftly. 'By clamping down on the big men, the developers who care for nothing else but making money. And as I said in my article, by limiting the size of craft and clearing the banks of gaudy houseboats. And who's to have the say? The planning authorities and the river authorities, of course.'

'But that's not the complete answer, is it?' Tony chimed in. 'What *about* people like Lance that you mentioned? Would you stop them developing their own business? You talk of limiting this and banning the other. It sounds to me like dictatorship.'

But Lee had an answer for everything. 'There simply have to be rules for the safeguard of the majority,' he insisted. 'Surely you can see that?'

Millie's attention was wandering now. She was looking across at the bar and sitting next to her, Kate glanced in the same direction to see a policeman standing there. He was asking about something and appeared to be looking straight in their direction.

'What does he want, I wonder?' murmured Millie.

Kate shook her head. Then the policeman made his way over to them.

He leaned over the table his face grave, and spoke to Kate.

'I'm afraid there's been an accident, Miss Martham. It's your father. He's been taken to hospital and detained.'

CHAPTER IX

Kate caught her breath sharply. 'Is—is he badly injured?' She pushed back her chair.

'It was a pretty bad smash-up, miss. The driver of the other car was killed.'

For a moment the room slipped sideways, and Kate felt a singing noise in her ears.

'Steady, Kate.' It was Lee's voice. 'Sit down for a minute, then I'll run you to the hospital.'

'No, no, I'm all right. I must go. I've got my car outside.'

'You're not driving yourself,' Lee said firmly. 'Come along.'

'Would you like me to come with you, Kate?' asked Lance.

But Kate shook her head and allowed Lee to lead her towards the door, the policeman following them.

Outside, Lee asked the constable which hospital Mr Martham had been taken to, then opened the door of his car and gently pushed Kate into it.

'Try not to worry, Kate,' he said as he started the engine. 'I'll have you there just as quickly as I possibly can.'

Kate tried to answer him, but couldn't. Her throat was dry and she felt sick with anxiety. She thought of her father unconscious or in pain and before she could do anything about it great sobs began to shake her and tears overflowed from her eyes.

'Oh, Lee—suppose—suppose—'

Swiftly, Lee put out a hand to her. 'Have courage, Kate. He'll be in the best possible hands, I'm sure. Put your hand in my pocket. You'll find a clean handkerchief in there.'

She felt comforted and dried her eyes with his big white handkerchief. At a traffic light he turned and took a good look at her, giving her an encouraging smile.

'Feeling a little better now?'

She nodded. 'It couldn't have been Father's fault. He always drives so carefully.'

He nodded and started the car in motion again. 'That's the damnable part about road accidents. The innocent suffer as well as the guilty. But your father might not be badly hurt, Kate. It happens that way sometimes. The occupants of one car are badly injured, the other party not at all—or only slightly.'

Lee drove as fast as he could and they arrived at the hospital much quicker than Kate would have done driving herself.

Her father's injuries were serious. After a long wait and a few words with the Sister, she was allowed to see him for a few minutes, but he was unconscious and his face covered with abrasions.

Afterwards the casualty officer spoke to her. 'We have to operate, Miss Martham. There are internal injuries. As well as that he has dislocation of the right shoulder and a fracture of the right tibia and fibula, so he'll be in hospital for some weeks.'

'Will he be all right?' Kate asked fearfully. 'He— he didn't know me.'

'Well, he is unconscious, of course. But as far as we can see at the moment there are no serious injuries to the brain. But we shall watch him carefully, you can be sure of that.'

'Can I stay?'

But the doctor shook his head. 'I wouldn't if I were you. We shall send for you if necessary, I assure you and you can ring in any time you like. Go home now and ring in about a couple of hours' time. Then go to bed and come and see him in the morning. Who is the man with you? A relative?'

'No, a—friend—neighbour. There's only me—and Father.'

The doctor gave her a kindly pat. 'Well, try not to worry, Miss Martham. We shall look after him for you as well as we possibly can, you can be sure of that.'

Lee had been having a word with Sister. He took Kate gently by the arm and led her back to his car.

'I'm glad you've decided to be sensible and not hang about. There wouldn't have been anything you could do. He'll need you most later on when he's conscious.'

'Lee, you do think he's going to be all right?'

He put his arm about her shoulders. 'I'm sure of it.'

She drew comfort from him, but tears came into her eyes again as she saw her father lying there, his eyes closed, his face covered with cuts and abrasions, knowing the pain he would be enduring. She simply could not get him out of her mind.

When they arrived home Lee came into the house with her. 'Mother will come and stay with you,' he said. 'You mustn't be alone. If I could use your phone?'

She nodded and stood rather helplessly in the hall while he dialled the number. He gave her an encouraging smile.

'Go and put the kettle on, Kate, and make some tea. I could do with a cup myself. And I'm sure you could.'

She did as she was told and the small task helped to occupy her mind a little.

About five minutes later Jane Thornton drove up in her own small car, carrying an overnight bag.

'My dear, what a terrible thing to have happened! You must be pretty nearly out of your mind. Come along, let's all have a cup of tea, then if you'll show me where the room is I'll make the bed up myself while you get into yours. Lee will ring the hospital for you later.'

By the time they had drunk their tea an hour had passed already since they had left the hospital. Lee offered to go to the Wherry to pick up Kate's car. On enquiring when she had eaten last, Jane suggested a light supper, and managed to keep Kate from worrying too much until it was time to ring the hospital. When Lee returned with her car he also brought a sleeping bag from his house.

'I'm sleeping on your sofa tonight,' he announced. 'I don't think it's the least likely, but if you *should* be called to the hospital urgently I shall be here to drive you.'

Kate barely knew how to thank them both. But she insisted on making up her father's bed with clean linen for him.

They were having supper when they were startled by the ringing of the telephone. Kate's heart contracted sharply and she felt every vestige of colour leave her face.

'I'll answer it,' Lee said.

He went swiftly into the hall and Kate followed him, her knees trembling. Lee spoke into the instrument once or twice, then turned to Kate.

'It's all right. It's Lance. Do you want to have a word with him?'

Kate almost laughed with relief as she took the instrument from Lee and spoke to Lance.

'You frightened me to death,' she told him. 'I thought it was the hospital ringing.'

'Sorry,' Lance said. 'How are you making out, Kate? Is there anything I can do? And how *is* your father?'

She gave him the news and told him that Lee and his mother were staying the night with her.

'That's very decent of them. You're quite happy

about it, are you? I've never met his mother.'

She assured him she was glad to have them. Lance said he would ring or call to see her the following day, then they rang off.

When she went back into the dining room Lee eyed her keenly, but made no comment. Later, when two hours had elapsed since leaving the hospital, he telephoned.

'It's as good as we can expect, Kate,' he told her when he replaced the receiver. 'Your father has had his operation and he's back in bed. The op. was successful and he's had a sedative. His leg and arm are in splints and they think the concussion is only slight. So off you go to bed and Mother'll bring you up a drink and a couple of sleeping tablets.'

She tried to thank him, but couldn't find the words. Lee put his hand momentarily on her head, then propelled her gently towards the stairs.

Worried though she was, Kate was so worn out she succumbed to the effect of Jane's sleeping tablets fairly quickly, and was awakened the next morning by Jane holding out a cup of tea.

'I hope you don't mind my making myself at home,' she said.

Kate sat up. 'Heavens, no. But I should have been doing this for *you*. Did you sleep well?'

Jane nodded. 'And you?'

'Flat out, thanks to your sleeping tablets.' She glanced at her bedside clock. 'I must ring the hospital as soon as possible.'

Jane smiled. 'Lee has already rung for you. Your father has had a fairly comfortable night and is conscious this morning.'

Kate sank back. 'Oh, thank goodness for that.' She sniffed as the delicious smell of bacon drifted upstairs. 'Are you cooking breakfast?'

'Lee is.'

'Oh, but he mustn't. This is terrible. I must get up.'

Jane laughed and moved towards the door. 'Don't worry, my dear. Just take your time. As long as you don't mind Lee making himself at home in your kitchen. He always cooks breakfast on Sunday mornings.'

Kate sat back and sipped her tea. If only circumstances were different! How lovely it would have been to have Lee here, cooking breakfast, taking command.

As soon as she had drunk her tea she washed and dressed quickly and went downstairs. The table was set for breakfast in the kitchen, coffee was percolating, and Lee was at the cooker forking bacon out of the pan, one of her aprons around his waist to protect his clothes.

'Lee, this is terrible—' she said again. 'You shouldn't be doing this.'

'Why not? Do you think women are the only ones who can cook?'

Kate could not resist a smile. 'The apron suits you, anyway.'

'Thanks. One egg or two?'

'Good heavens! Only one.'

He had already made toast. Kate put some milk on to heat for the coffee.

'Thanks for ringing the hospital,' she said to him. 'I'm most awfully grateful to both you and your mother.'

'Think nothing of it,' he told her. 'Did you manage to get some sleep?'

She said she had, and then Jane came down and they sat down to breakfast. Lee insisted on driving her to the hospital and was adamant when she tried to protest.

'You're not putting me out in the least,' he said. 'When we know for certain that your father is out of danger, then you can drive yourself.' He added: 'Did Lance say whether he was coming over?'

'He said he would ring or call some time today, and asked if there was anything he could do.'

'What about the business?' Lee asked her. 'It's going to be difficult managing without your father, I imagine, especially as you'll be going frequently to the hospital. If Lance—'

But Kate shook her head. 'I can't let Lance neglect his own work. I shall just have to manage. The staff are all very good.'

Jane said quietly: 'Kate, I hope you'll let me stay with you while your father's in hospital. That is, unless you have another friend who—'

Kate shook her head. 'You've been very, very sweet and kind, Mrs Thornton. There's no one I'd rather have than you, but I don't want to impose—'

'How can you be imposing when I've offered? And I *want* to stay. After all, quite apart from anything else, we *are* your nearest neighbours.'

Kate thanked her again. She did not want to refer to the day when her father ordered Lee off, but she thought it extremely good of him to have stayed last night under the circumstances. Jane insisted on them leaving the washing-up to her, and Lee and Kate set off for the hospital.

'I'll wait outside for you,' he said when they arrived. 'I'd better not come in at this stage. Perhaps later you might ask him if I can see him.'

Her father was drowsy, but recognized her. Almost the first words he said were:

'Kate, I'm sorry about this.'

She kissed him. 'Sorry, Father? It isn't your fault you're in this predicament.'

But he was clearly troubled. 'It wasn't my fault if the other man was killed, but if my mind had been fully concentrated on my driving I might have taken better avoiding action.'

Kate put her hand on his arm. What had been on her father's mind? What was it that was bothering him so much?

'Father, you're not to worry. Just get well.'

'Not to worry? It's going to be difficult not to, knowing I've left you to carry on that business on your own.'

'I shan't *be* on my own. You forget we've got a perfectly good staff.'

His head stirred restlessly on the pillow. 'Are you trying to tell me that one of us is redundant? That you can manage perfectly well without me?'

'Of course I'm not, Father. Don't be silly. I shall miss you like—like nobody's business, you know that. But it won't be for long—only a week or two.'

But he was not to be so easily consoled. 'There's another thing, Kate. I don't like the idea of your being alone in the house. Could you get one of your friends to stay with you, or one of the women from the café?'

Kate mentally crossed her fingers. 'Mrs Thornton stayed with me last night, Father, and she offered to stay for the rest of the time while you're here.' She thought she had better not mention Lee at this point.

To her relief he smiled. 'She did? Oh, good. Well, that's all right, then.'

He closed his eyes, and she sat there for a minute or two, not sure whether he had gone to sleep or was unconscious. But after a little while he opened them again.

'Hello, Kate. You still here? I thought you'd gone.'

She rose. 'I will go now, Father, and I'll come and see you again this evening if they'll let me.'

She kissed him and his eyes were closed again before she left the room. She sought out the Ward Sister who told her that her father was still slightly concussed, but with rest and quiet and freedom from anxiety he would make a good recovery.

'He still has to recover from the operation, of course. And his fractures will take some weeks to unite. But we don't think there's any brain damage apart from shock, so—'

'Thank you, Sister. May I come again this evening?'

'Come as often as you like, but he should be out of immediate danger in a day or two.'

Lee eyed her anxiously when she rejoined him. 'How is he?' he asked.

She gave him the report on her father's physical condition, then went on:

'It niggles me— has done all the time, even for weeks before his accident—that Father hasn't been happy lately. He thinks if he'd been concentrating better he might have avoided the accident.'

'Is he worried about the business?'

'I shouldn't think so. We're doing as well as we ever did.'

'It can't be anything to do with those articles of mine —I hope,' offered Lee, has face grave.

'Oh no, Lee,' she said impulsively. 'He was angry and all that, I know, but—'

Lee set the car towards home again. 'Did you tell him I stayed at your house last night?'

She shook her head. 'Only that your mother did.'

'What did he say?'

'He was very pleased.'

'Well, that's something.' Then he said: 'By the way, did you tell him you'd been out to dinner with me the other evening?'

'I told him the next morning—and shortly afterwards he read that latest article of yours.'

'Oh dear! And what did he say to that?'

'He blew his top, naturally. He was angry with me and he was angry with you, but most of all with you.'

Lee frowned. 'I'm sorry if I've made things difficult

174

for you and annoyed your father, but I have to write
about what I believe in. You do see that?'

'I see it. But Father feels you're getting at us. He
pointed out—and rightly, in my opinion—that but for
the revenue which comes from hire craft, and by that I
mean the licence fees which are paid to the river
authority, half the rivers would be silted up, especially
the upper reaches and the smaller ones. The same
applies to the Broads. And silted-up water is not a
pretty sight. It certainly isn't beautiful.'

'He has a point there,' Lee conceded.

'Then I wish to goodness you'd find a way of letting
Father know,' exploded Kate.

'I might—if he'd give me the chance,' he answered
stiffly.

He drove in silence after that, and Kate stared at the
road ahead, her mind a mixture of emotions and worries,
large and small.

'Lee, I'm sorry,' she said at last. 'I shouldn't have
spoken to you like that—especially after all you've done.'

'Neither thanks nor apologies are necessary, Kate,' he
answered in a flat voice.

Kate felt rebuffed, shut out. For a minute or two
she battled with her hurt feelings, her love for him, and
the whole turmoil of her emotions. Then she burst out:

'But I *want* to thank you! Why shouldn't I? And
why shouldn't you accept my thanks? It's been wonderful to have someone to lean on, to—'

He turned the car into the drive of her home and there
was Lance just getting out of his car.

'All right, Kate,' Lee said as if he were pacifying a
child. 'I'll accept your thanks. But it rather looks
as though you'll have someone else to lean on from now
on. I'll just go in and have a word with Mother, then
beetle off home. I've got some work to do.'

He got swiftly out of the car and Kate's thanks to him

for driving her to the hospital died in her throat. He spoke briefly to Lance, then went into the house.

Lance looked at her anxiously as she got out of the car. 'You look a bit miserable, Kate. I hope your father's all right.'

With an effort she told him all the news. 'The Sister said he'd be out of danger in a few days, but I shall go and see him again tonight. I shall go twice a day until he's out of danger, anyway. Then just in the evenings, I expect.'

'I could run you to the hospital tonight. And perhaps I could see him. Father would like to see him too, but he'll be giving you a ring and checking with you first. Both Mother and Dad are terribly cut up about the accident. Father rang the hospital both last night and this morning.'

Kate smiled. 'Thanks, Lance. It's nice to have friends at times like this. And I'll be glad of you to run me to the hospital tonight. I could drive myself of course, but—' She broke off, thinking of what her father had told her.

'Not while you're so worried,' Lance told her.

Lee came out of the house again, nodded to them, then got into his car and drove away. Lance gazed after him thoughtfully.

'You know, he's not such a bad bloke, after all, is he?' I liked the way he faced us all last night and was willing to argue the thing out and listen. And there was a lot in what he said. Mind you, I daren't say so to Father. The older generation are so intolerant.'

'About some things, perhaps,' agreed Kate. 'About others, their offspring, for instance, as you've said yourself, they're inclined to treat us like children. But then I suppose we all get a little confused in our thinking at times. Such as when the emotions are involved.'

Lance grinned. 'What philosophizing! But I expect

176

you're right. By the way, Millie's come round all at once. She seemed to think I stood up to Lee Thornton magnificently.'

Kate smiled. Dear, simple, easy-going Lance. He was very sweet and she hoped Millie would make him happy.

'There have been quite a number of telephone calls enquiring about your father,' Jane told her when she went indoors. 'I've written them all down on the pad.'

Lance stayed for coffee, then went home, arranging to call for her about six-thirty that evening. Jane was cooking lunch.

'I hope you don't mind. I found your little joint in the fridge. We can share ours tomorrow. Oh, and by the way, somebody came wanting to hire a dayboat. I didn't know what I was supposed to do, so I gave them one, took the licence number and the name and also the name and address of the hirer. Was that all right?'

Kate hugged her. 'Perfectly. Thanks very much. I honestly don't know what I'd have done without you. Lee, too,' she added, her expression clouding over.

Jane's look softened. 'Lee on his high horse again? He wants to help, but he doesn't want to intrude. Seeing Lance made him wonder whether he should fade out.'

'But why? Lance is a very old friend. I don't know why Lee should feel like that. I've been very grateful to him, but I—don't want to be a trouble to anyone.'

Jane's hand shot out to touch her arm. 'Kate, don't say things like that. Try to bear with Lee. He—has his problems. I—can't tell what they are, naturally, they're too personal, but—'

To Kate, the implication was obvious. She was sure it was something to do with either Millie or Miss Wainwright.

'I think I understand,' she murmured.

Jane eyed her keenly. 'Kate, do you mind if I ask

you a personal question?'

'Of course not?'

'Are you in love with Lance?'

Kate shook her head swiftly.

'Lee is under the impression that you are,' Jane said.

'I expect a lot of people are,' Kate answered, and made an excuse to go up to her room.

She did not stay there long. In the summer when the weather was fine—and it was now early summer—the boatyard could be quite busy on Sundays. People would turn out, especially after lunch, for a run in their cars and call at the café for a cup of tea, sit beside the Broad or stroll around looking at the different boats moored there, and in general enjoy a pleasant Sunday afternoon out. Others would take out a rowing boat or launch for an hour or two. A skeleton staff was employed—at double pay—but Sundays often meant that either Kate or her father were kept fairly busy. In the very height of the season and on bank holidays both would be ' on duty'. Today Kate was kept busy until the time came for her to visit her father. Lee appeared briefly for lunch, and on learning that Lance was running her to the hospital, disappeared again, saying he would keep an eye on things while she was away.

Between anxiety about her father and heartache over Lee, Kate felt as though lead weights were pressing down on her from all sides. She only heard half of what Lance was saying as he drove her into Norwich. Fortunately, she found her father had made some improvement since the morning, but he was still worried about the business.

'Don't you worry, Mr Martham,' Lance said. 'We'll all rally round, you can be sure of that.'

But on the way home Kate said to him, 'You mustn't neglect your own business, Lance. I can manage, really I can. I shan't be able to have much time off, naturally, but I shan't mind that. In fact, I'll be glad to be kept busy.'

Lance was dubious, but gave way. 'That may be, but if you do want any help or need someone to stand in for you while you visit your father don't hesitate to pick the phone up, will you?'

She promised she wouldn't, but simply could not see how any of her friends in the boathire business could possibly spare the time to help her, especially on Saturdays when she would probably need an extra hand.

By Tuesday her father was out of danger with regard to the concussion and had recovered from the worst of the operation. Kate then confined her visits to the evenings.

'Could I come with you, do you think?' Jane asked her about mid-week. 'I mean, do you think your father would mind?'

'Mind? He'll be delighted, I'm sure,' Kate told her eagerly. 'And it will do him a lot of good. Every time I go he seems to do nothing but worry about how I'm managing. You'll be able to talk to him about something else.'

Jane's visit cheered her father up immensely. 'Come again, won't you?' he asked as they left him.

And Jane did, sometimes even dropping in to see him while she was shopping in town, taking him books and periodicals, doing small items of shopping for him and keeping him supplied with little luxuries like fruit and cakes.

'Lee, why don't you drop in to see him one day?' she suggested towards the week-end. 'I'm sure he'd be pleased to see you.'

'He'd be more likely to order me out of his sight,' Lee answered wryly.

'Nonsense,' Jane asserted. 'He's the nicest, mildest of men when you get to know him, isn't he, Kate?'

Kate smiled. 'He has his moments, but you seem to

have found his best side, anyway.'

Kate had her doubts about her father being pleased to see Lee, but on their next visit to the hospital Jane said to him:

'Lee says he'd like to come and see you. Will that be all right?'

Kate held her breath. Jane appeared to have got to know her father awfully well. She wouldn't have dared make the suggestion to him herself.

'Of course it will,' he answered, to her surprise. Then he added: 'But on one condition. That he keeps off the subject of the Broads.'

'I'll tell him,' Jane promised.

Though Kate had barely seen Lee during the week, on Saturday he lent a hand with the change-over, helping cruisers to come in to moor, giving a hand with luggage, showing people to their boats, giving them a push-off and in general helping in a thousand and one different ways. Kate thought of her father and wondered what he would say if he could see Lee making himself useful around his boatyard. But perhaps he wouldn't mind. It was extraordinary, she thought, the influence Jane seemed to be having on her father.

'When are you thinking of visiting Father?' she asked Lee when, all at once, it seemed, she found herself standing alone with him in the quiet and peace of the evening. All the hired craft had gone, there were none as yet from other boatyards and the setting sun was shedding a soft mellow light and lengthening the shadows over the water.

'Perhaps tomorrow—or Monday,' he answered.

He lit his pipe, and the easy companionship, the quiet stillness of the evening was almost more heavenly, more poignant than Kate could bear. *This, oh, this for the rest of her life.*

'I think I shall tell your father that I've been giving you a hand,' Lee said, breaking the silence. 'I don't want to upset him, of course, but at the same time, I wouldn't like to be doing anything he would disapprove of. But you don't seem to be getting much help from anywhere else, if you don't mind my saying so.'

' How can they? Lance or any of them, I mean. Saturday is such a busy day for them all.'

' I suppose so. But has anyone offered to relieve you so that you can take a day off? Or even a half day?'

' I only have to pick up the phone and ask,' she told him. ' But I don't want to be relieved. I'd rather keep busy.'

' But why? Your father's out of danger now.'

Why? How could she answer him when he himself was her reason for preferring to fill every moment with work and responsibility?

Lee took his pipe out of his mouth and eyed it thoughtfully.

' I could look after things now if you want to go along to the Wherry as usual. Lance will be there, I imagine.'

She could have wept. Didn't he know that all she wanted was to stay here with him, to drink in the peace of the evening, to talk to him, to draw closer to him? But it was blantantly obvious that he did not want her company.

' Thanks, I will,' she said, and swung away from him into the house.

But she didn't go to the Wherry. She couldn't. She changed and drove to the hospital to see her father. He was surprised to see her.

' I didn't expect to see you, Katie,' he said. ' How'd you make out today? I don't suppose you got any help from anyone.'

She had no option but to tell him the truth. ' As a matter of fact, Father, Lee Thornton gave me a hand.'

' What?' he shot out, his eyes widening.

' I—I hope you don't mind. He—offered, and of

course Lance and everyone would be too busy.'

He subsided. 'Well—no, I don't mind exactly. I'm just surprised, that's all, in view of the way I ordered him off. I suppose there must be some good in him with a mother like Jane.'

Kate's brows raised a little. 'So you call her Jane now?'

He shot her a swift look. 'It's the fashion, isn't it? We older people are not so stuffy as you youngsters seem to think.'

Kate took a deep breath. '*Father!* In between what you call the older people and the youngsters, there's another generation which you seem to forget. Mine. We're *not* youngsters.'

'You're forever quibbling, Kate. But I take your point. Anyway you can hardly keep on calling someone '' Mrs '' all the time when you're around the same age and they're being so friendly. I must say she's being a very good friend to both of us. Pity about that son of hers, but you seem to get along with him. If only somebody could knock a bit of sense into him about the boat-hire business !'

'Perhaps if you both modified your ideas?' suggested Kate mildly.

'What are you talking about?' He glared and waved an accusing finger at her. But she laughed and took hold of it.

'Stop shouting or you'll get me turned out ! Anyway, I think he's coming to see you tomorrow, so for goodness' sake don't quarrel with him.'

He reminded her that it took two people to make a quarrel. 'I shan't start anything if he doesn't.'

As Lee had promised to keep off the subject of the Broads, Kate thought it would be all right.

On her way home she thought how ironical it was that at last it looked as though Lee and her father might at least agree to differ about certain things, if only for Jane's sake. Ironical because it would not make the slightest difference to the way Lee felt about Kate herself. And as if fate were anxious to emphasize the fact, the very next day Joanna Wainwright drove up and Lee went off somewhere with her for the day.

Lee's visit to her father was successful, though neither was very communicative with regard to what they had talked about. 'This, that and the other,' was Eric Martham's version, and 'Various things,' was all that could be gleaned from Lee.

'Well, at least they didn't come to blows,' Jane said drily.

Kate smiled, but she felt as though her heart was slowly breaking. Perhaps, she thought, when her father had completely recovered from his accident, she could persuade him to have a housekeeper and get right away somewhere. Yet how could she? Even with a housekeeper her father would still be lonely. Her only hope was that with her father back in harness, she would not see so much of Lee. As it was, during the remaining weeks of her father's stay in hospital, although he no longer slept at the house, he helped in some way at the boatyard every day, and also paid several more visits to her father.

One day when Jane returned from one of her visits she seemed unusually preoccupied.

'Father in good spirits?' Kate asked her.

Jane frowned and smiled almost at the same time. 'Oh yes. He thinks he might be ready for home in about another week.'

'That's good,' answered Kate, giving her a puzzled look.

Jane went over to the window and stood looking out in a way which suggested that there was something on her mind.

'Anything wrong?' Kate asked her.

Jane shook her head. 'Not really.' She turned, trim and neat in a well-fitting blouse and skirt, her dark hair soft and shining, her attractive face serious.

'Kate, I must tell you. Your father has asked me to marry him.'

CHAPTER X

Kate's eyes widened in surprise. For a moment she just stared at Jane, not quite knowing what to say. But Jane spoke again.

'You don't look very pleased about it,' she remarked.

'I'm a bit staggered, that's all. He—he really meant it, did he?'

'I think so.'

'What did you say? Are you going to?'

Jane moved to an armchair and pulled another one around.

'Come and sit down, Kate, and let's talk.'

Kate sat down, thinking about her father and some of the things he had said. He had been attracted to Jane from the first time he had seen her. She remembered now. And yet he seemed fanatically devoted to the memory of Kate's mother.

'Kate—' Jane began, 'I think your father is a very wonderful person. When I'm with him I feel happy and at peace. He feels the same when he's with me. I'd like to marry him—I can think of nothing which would give me greater happiness, and I think your father would be happy, too. We would be doubly happy if you and Lee approved of the idea.'

At the mention of Lee, Kate wanted to burst out crying. It was incredible, heartbreakingly incredible that her father and his mother could fall in love, and yet Lee—she caught sight of Jane's anxious face and rose swiftly, brushing her thoughts aside.

She took Jane's hands in hers and kissed her cheek. 'I can't speak for Lee, but *I* approve, very much indeed, and I'm sure you'll both be extremely happy.'

Relief showed in Jane's face. 'Bless you, Kate. You

and I are good friends, I know, but you might not have liked the idea of having me as a stepmother. Not that I shall want you to think of me as that. I shall want you to go on regarding me as a friend.'

Kate went back to her chair. 'Does—Lee know?'

Jane shook her head. 'Not yet. There'll be much to talk about, to arrange. I think your father and I might put off actually getting married until—until Lee is—well, at least engaged.'

Kate felt a sudden return of the ache which now seemed constantly in her throat. She left her chair swiftly.

'Jane, do you mind if I—take a walk? Just to think about things.'

'Of course not.'

But once outside, Kate did what was for her, the natural thing. She stepped into the well of the *Aerial* and hoisted sail. At first, the movement of the half-decker was sluggish. The craft moved along reluctantly, the sails barely filling out, but the leaden movement matched the heaviness of her heart. She was pleased about Jane and her father, of course, but their marriage would make Lee and herself part of the same family, and she was in love with him. How could she possibly bear it, more especially if he were married to someone else? One thing was certain. Her father would not be alone now. She would be free to get right away. It was the only thing she could do.

Out in the open river she went in the direction which gave her a slightly more brisk following wind, and let the *Aerial* go its own way, thinking of her father and his moods of the past months. Had this been his problem all along? The need to marry again, the need for a companion his own age? Perhaps that was even the reason why he had been anxious to see herself married and settled down, married to Lance. Not consciously maybe, but subconsciously.

The next time she went to visit her father he was already a different man, serene and contented.

'I hope you don't mind, Katie,' he said. 'But I knew you liked Jane and was sure you'd be happy with her in the house until you find a man of your own. And that son of hers is a jolly decent type. I think we shall be a very happy family.'

Kate nodded and kissed him. 'Father, I'm glad, tremendously glad, and I think you'll both be very happy indeed.'

'Bless you, Kate. I'm afraid I haven't been any too easy to live with of late. All at once I began to miss your mother afresh and nothing seemed right. I guess a man isn't meant to live without a partner. It wasn't too bad when you were little and I was still building up the business, but—'

'I understand, Father.'

Eric Martham looked at his daughter anxiously. 'You're the only one I'm worried about now. I want to see you with a good husband and a home of your own. Not that I don't want you at home—' he added hastily.

'I know, Father.'

'Jane's a bit anxious about Lee, too. She doesn't want to leave him in that house to fend for himself. But I gather he hopes to get married himself pretty soon.'

Kate stood up quickly. 'I really ought to be going, Father. It won't be long before you'll be home now, then we can talk everything over and make plans.'

She kissed him and went out swiftly, a mist of tears blurring her path. If Lee married Joanna both of them would be part of the family. She must get away somewhere soon.

At last the day arrived for her father's discharge from hospital. Kate and Jane drove to the hospital together to bring him home, leaving Lee to take care of things at the house and boatyard.

'Will you stay on with us for a while?' Kate asked her on the way, 'or would you rather go home until the wedding?'

'Oh, I shall go home, I think. After tonight, at any rate, if that's all right with you. There are quite a number of things I want to do at Thornton House. How soon your father and I get married depends on Lee's plans.'

'I see.'

'Yours too, of course,' Jane said, giving her a sidelong glance.

'Oh, don't worry about me,' Kate said swiftly. 'It's just possible that I might go away for a while, but I don't want to say anything to Father for the time being.'

Jane said nothing. She sat in thoughtful silence for the rest of the journey to the hospital.

Eric Martham walked to the car on crutches, accompanied by a nurse. He had lost the tan which his outdoor life had given him but had gained rather than lost weight, owing to his enforced lack of exercise, but he looked enormously happy.

He insisted on sitting in the back of the car with Jane, and the two of them laughed and joked like children as they found the best way of arranging themselves to accommodate his leg. In the end he rested his injured leg on Jane's lap while Kate had the crutches in the front.

'You don't mind acting as chauffeur, do you, Kate?' he asked cheerfully.

'Of course not,' she answered, and caught a glimpse of their hands linked tightly together.

When they arrived home Lee was waiting to hand her father out of the car and into the house.

'My goodness, but it's wonderful to be home again!'

he exclaimed, looking all around.

'Shall I set a chair by the window for you?' Lee asked.

'Chair by the window? Lord, no. I'm going outside. I want to see what everything looks like.'

'Father, be careful,' Kate said swiftly.

'Don't worry, I'll take care of him,' said Jane. 'Come on then, Eric. I know you're dying to see the Broad again.'

Kate watched his progress anxiously for a moment, but he had acquired a fair competence with his crutches in hospital before his discharge.

'Do you mind someone else taking care of your father?' queried Lee at her side.

'Not your mother, at any rate,' she answered.

'You're happy about the parents, then, are you?'

Oddly enough Lee and Kate had not discussed their parents' engagement at all. They had had very little private conversation during the past week or so. Unconsciously, Kate had avoided close contact with him and when Lee had not been helping in and around the boatyard he had been out on his own affairs.

But before she could answer she heard Lance's voice, and the next moment he came into the room.

'I was just passing—thought I'd look in. Your father home, then?'

Kate turned. 'Hello, Lance. Come and have a word with him. And I don't think you've been introduced to Jane yet, have you?'

His presence was a relief. Kate went outside with him and told him about her father's engagement.

Lance was staggered. 'Good lord!' Then he caught a sight of Jane's face as she turned to help her father on to a seat. 'You don't mean that's her?'

'Yes. Oh, but of course, you've never actually seen her, have you?'

Lance stopped and stared. ' You mean to tell me that she's Lee Thornton's mother?'

Kate eyed him with amusement. ' I couldn't believe it at first either.'

But to her surprise Lance threw back his head and laughed aloud. ' But I *have* seen her before. I've seen her in Thornton's car. I mistook her for one of his—his girl-friends.'

Kate laughed too. ' You mean she's the attractive " mature woman " you said you'd seen him with when you were accusing him of being a flirt?'

Lance nodded. ' I'm afraid the man has been sadly misjudged. Millie was telling me the other day that he never even asked her out once. She only pushed herself on to him to try to make me jealous. But I must go and have a word with both of them, then push off.'

When he had gone Kate went into the house again, still smiling at Lance's mistake. She met Lee in the doorway.

' You look happy about something,' he said. ' You and Lance made it up?'

She looked at him calmly, without any effort to hide the way she felt about him. The laughter with Lance had done something to her, snapped her into life.

' I think perhaps it's time we had a talk, Lee. We seem to have a few misunderstandings about each other. Lance and I never quarrelled, so we've nothing to make up.'

' But you were in love once and unhappy on his account. I saw you one evening myself—wrapped in each other's arms. And you've certainly been unhappy about something.'

She shook her head. ' You've been jumping to a lot of conclusions. Lance and I thought we were in love at one time, but discovered it was something we had drifted into. Lance is going to marry Millie.'

'And you don't mind?'

'Of course not. Why do you take so much convincing?'

He gave her such a fierce incredulous look, she backed away from him and came up against the frame of the door. He took a step towards her and imprisoned her there.

'How can I take a lot of convincing when you've only just told me?' he demanded. 'And if I've jumped to conclusions, well, so have a lot of other people, and for the simple reason that you've done your best to convince everybody that you *were* going to marry him. Lance being financed in a boathire business by both your fathers, you going round there—always together. What other conclusion could anyone reach?'

She looked at him wide-eyed. 'If you were all that interested you could have asked me,' she retorted.

'Asked you? Heaven knows I tried, but you were like a prickly pear. I didn't seem to be able to get near you.'

She closed her eyes momentarily, trying to adjust her mind to this sudden, unexpected, extremely personal contact with him. Was there anything in it? Did he really care or was he just—

Then her heart seemed to stop beating as she felt her lips covered by something soft and warm.

'Lee—'

She opened her eyes to look straight into his. 'Lee, please don't do that unless—unless you mean it.'

'I don't make a habit of doing this kind of thing if I don't mean it,' he answered softly, kissing her once more.

'But—but—' she said incredulously, 'what about Joanna Wainwright?'

'What about her?'

'Aren't you—going to marry her?'

'I am not,' he answered emphatically. 'Now who's jumping to conclusions? You're the only woman I want to marry.'

She couldn't believe it. Her lips trembled and tears she could no longer hide filled her eyes.

'But—but, Lee, I thought—you thought I was too young.'

'You thought I thought,' he mocked gently. 'Well, perhaps I did at first, but oh, my darling Kate, I love you.'

'Lee, oh, Lee—'

Swiftly her arms went around his neck and simultaneously he caught her to him, murmuring all kinds of things she had never dared hope to hear, then covering her lips with his again in a long, hard kiss.

'Lee, I love you. That's why I was so miserable, because I thought—' she uttered when she could breathe again.

He possessed her lips utterly and silenced her. He took her hand. 'Let's go and tell the parents. We'll make it a double wedding. It will be quite unique, I should think.'

There was hardly any need to say anything to either Jane or Kate's father.

'Hello, you two,' said Jane, glancing at their entwined fingers and smiling calmly as if she quite expected it.

And from father: 'You know, Kate, I've been thinking. I think we'll get rid of those houseboats. I'm going to need a little more leisure in the future, and besides, they spoil the view.'